A LISTING

OF THE WORKS OF

ROBERT NATHAN

PUBLISHED BY ALFRED A. KNOPF

WILL BE FOUND AT THE END

OF THIS VOLUME.

The
Elixir

The Elixir

by

ROBERT NATHAN

NEW YORK : Alfred · A · Knopf

1 9 7 1

THIS IS A BORZOI BOOK
PUBLISHED BY ALFRED A. KNOPF, INC.

International Standard Book Number: 0–394–47175–X
Library of Congress Catalog Card Number: 73–154936

Manufactured in the United States of America

First Edition

to Anne, of course

For there bee an Elixir Amyranth, the same being very potent and of great Mysterie, which enableth a man to see the world spread out before him like unto a tapestrie, both today and yesterday. And this Elixir is called by some Amyranth, and by some, Love.

Bernard of Trèves (trans. John Dee)

Speak your truth quietly & clearly; and listen to others, even the dull & ignorant; they too have their story. . . . Neither be cynical about love; for in the face of all aridity & disenchantment it is perennial as the grass. . . . You are a child of the universe, no less than the trees & the stars; you have a right to be here. And whether or not it is clear to you, no doubt the universe is unfolding as it should. Therefore be at peace with God, whatever you conceive Him to be. . . . With all its sham, drudgery & broken dreams, it is still a beautiful world. Be careful. Strive to be happy.

Anon.—Baltimore, 1692

The
Elixir

1

It was already evening when I approached Stonehenge, and the tourist bus was pulling away for its return to Salisbury. It had been a long and on the whole a boring drive from Avebury; in the gentle twilight the great circle of prehistoric stones rose above the plain like misty towers of a distant town seen on the world's rim.

It had been a warm day in mid-June, but with the sun gone, the air had turned cool and soft. There was no sudden sunset; the light had drained quietly away, the sky fading to a faint rose and then to a cool green which lingered on and on.

The full moon rose, huge and golden, between the waiting monoliths, lighting a path through the inner trilithon to the altar stone; and slowly climbing higher, washed the circling stones in silver laced with inky shadows. A little mist crept upward from the ground; there was a cold smell of stone around me.

All was silent; stillness hung upon the air, a stillness not only of the night but of the spirit. There is nothing so silent as the past; it is even more mysterious than the future which lies open to the imagination, but the past is closed.

I was in the last week of my vacation: as an historian, I had been following the course of Arthur's campaigns; I had seen the ruins of old castles and older abbeys, and had come at last to Stonehenge, to the most distant history of all. Here, by this altar stone, they had buried the body of Ambrosius who was the last Roman Count of Britain. And even then, the stones were old and fallen. They were here when the Druids met in their magical ceremonies, when Boadicea led her chariots against the Romans.

Set here by whom? The Beaker people? The Battle-Axe people of the Wessex barrows? Where had they come from, these unknown builders?

Was it from the South, from Minoan Crete, from
a civilization older than Babylon, older than
Troy. . . ?

I opened the picnic supper I had ordered put
up for me at the inn in Avebury, and seating myself
on one of the fallen sarsen stones, started to munch
the bread and cheese, and to drink a little of the
wine. All England lay around me in the night, its
counties and shires, its ancient kingdoms; the
White Rose and the Red, Norman and Saxon and
beyond, Roman and Celt, the blue-woaded Iceni,
the wars won and lost, far off and forgotten. Distantly about me slumbered the Old Ones, their
bones long bleached in the lonely barrows, the
Corn-worshipers and Fire-Watchers; in churches
and ruined abbeys, Crusaders in their sepulchers,
mailed knights. . . . England was full of ghosts. I
thought of my quiet, day-to-day life in the small
New England college where I taught history. There
were no ghosts in Massachusetts.

I must have slept, for I was awakened by singing; and only half aware of it before I woke. I had
had an experience like that once before, in the re-
covery room of a hospital after an operation; only

half aware of my own being, and hearing almost as in a dream someone singing, distant and yet not far away.

I roused slowly to the reality of where I was. The moon had circled to the west, and the darkness was even blacker than before; it was cold, and the damp smell of stone hung in the air about me. And somebody was singing.

It was a girl's voice, or a woman's, curiously innocent, but a little sad. Or perhaps it only seemed so, in the night, and in that place, and the music being, besides, in a minor mode like so many of the songs today. She seemed to be lamenting a lost happiness, or a lost lover; as I listened, the song seemed vaguely familiar, I thought it was something I had heard before in another setting.

I must confess that for a moment I was frightened—or at least disquieted, and felt a quick rush of that mortal alarm one feels in the face of the unexpected and unnatural. But it was only momentary, and followed by a feeling of surprise and curiosity; the song, thin on the midnight air, seemed to have an unearthly sweetness, due more to the place itself perhaps, to the strange setting, than to its own natural beauty. I thought of the ancient

Druid mysteries, of Merlin imprisoned forever in his cave—or was it a tree?—by the nymph Nimue . . .

I hesitated a moment, and then rose and, still in shadow, moved quietly around the base of the altar stone in the direction of an area of moonlight from which the song appeared to be coming. I was not at all sure what I expected to find; I remember that I held my breath.

I found a young woman seated on the fallen roof stone of a trilithon, plucking at a guitar, and singing. She was dressed in a long gown, and wore a wreath of flowers in her hair. She seemed as startled to see me as I was to see her. "Oh!" she breathed, and half rose from her seat, holding the guitar before her like a shield. "Who . . . who are you?"

I was still fogged with sleep and with the cold. "You are not Nimue," I said stupidly.

Her face was in shadow, her hair hung like a waterfall over her shoulders, and in the moonlight appeared to be of a pale color, possibly silver but more likely gold. "I was asleep," I said, "and I heard you singing. I'm sorry if I frightened you."

"You did a bit," she admitted; and sat down

limply, the guitar in her lap. "I didn't know anyone was here."

"I didn't, either," I said.

She considered this, with her head tilted a little to one side. "Still," she said, "you must have been expecting someone, mustn't you?"

"Nimue," I said. "She was a witch, and the death of Merlin."

"I see," she said, "I'm sorry. Merlin was long ago, in Arthur's time."

"I know," I said. "I was hoping you weren't Nimue."

"I shouldn't think I could be," she said. "So you're not to worry.

"As a matter of fact," she declared, as though she had suddenly decided to confess, "my uncle is the Vicar of Saffron Orcas."

Never having heard of Saffron Orcas, I nodded politely. "It's a village," she explained. "In Dorset. You're an American, aren't you?"

"Yes."

"Well, that's all right then. I mean—you wouldn't know where it was."

"I'm afraid not," I said. "I've only been in England a little while."

She seemed reassured for some reason, and motioned to the stone slab on which she was seated. "Would you care to sit down?" she asked.

"Thank you," I said.

Seated beside her in the cold moonlight, I felt, to my surprise, both at ease, and curiously breathless. I shivered a little, and braced myself; was it the cold? Or was it something else, something I used to feel when I was young, when the mystery all around me was my own mystery, created just for me . . . trembling on the brink of revelation? Although I was scarcely within arm's reach of the girl, I was intensely aware of her; I could sense the softness and slenderness of her body. I could smell her fragrance, some kind of small-flower fragrance. . . . A young English girl with long golden hair, alone in the moonlight among the tumbled stones of an ancient race, singing to herself some long-ago, half-remembered melody . . .

"What was it you were singing?" I asked.

"Oh . . . I don't know, really. Something I made up . . . I think."

"It sounded familiar somehow—"

"It just came to me. Though I might have heard it on a gramophone record, I suppose. They all

The Elixir

sound the same, don't you think? The songs today?"

It was true; and yet, there had been something
about it . . . I didn't know what. Something curiously old-fashioned . . . antique almost, from another time.

She plucked a few notes from her guitar. "Are
you studying in England?" she asked. "Or are you
a tourist?"

I explained that I had been visiting as many
historic places as possible before returning to my
duties as a teacher in New England. I told her my
name—Robert Irwin, and she told me hers—
Niniane Mellers, though it seemed to me that she
hesitated a moment over the Mellers. "How did you
come?" I asked. "I saw no other car." She told me
that she had come with the bus—she called it the
charabanc—and that it had gone off without her. "I
thought that if I stayed the night, I might get a lift
to Saffron Orcas in the morning," she said. "In any
case, there was no help for it."

She admitted that she had had no supper, and I
brought out the remains of the bread and cheese
and wine. "Oh, lovely," she said, and sighed happily.

She ate like a hungry bird, delicate but greedy.
Her hands made milky arabesques in the moon-

light; she held the wine bottle above her head, and tilted her mouth to it like a bird; she peered at me like a bird, bright-eyed and mischievous, as though she had got the better of me somehow. I found myself watching her in a kind of delight; I was reminded of my friend Baggot, the novelist, who always said that he created his characters out of fog and rain and flowering bushes . . .

"What fun," she said.

(. . . and love and memory, but that seemed irrelevant at the moment.)

After she had finished the last of the wine, and had brushed the last crumb of bread from her lap, she appeared to grow restless, and after a while she asked, with an air of dejection,

"Do you mean to stay here all night?"

I explained that I had planned to watch the midsummer sunrise. "You see," I said, "Stonehenge is actually a sort of calendar, built by astronomer-mathematicians, to mark the equinoxes. The midsummer sun rises at that exact point in the trilithon on which all the other measurements depend."

I went on to admit that it had also probably been used for sacrifices to the god, "who in this case," I declared, "would have been the sun-god."

"The corn-god," she corrected.

She spoke so simply, yet firmly, that I glanced at her in surprise. She sat with her head thrown back, staring up at the sky, her long, slender white throat arched like a swan. "The sun will be coming up before long," she remarked.

She brought her head down, and turned to look at me, a child's look, both innocent and anxious. "Would you, do you think," she asked, "drive me to Salisbury afterwards? That is—if it weren't terribly out of your way."

"Of course," I said heartily. And I added, by way of reassurance,

"To Saffron Orcas if you like."

"Oh," she said, and seemed taken aback. "How lovely," she said.

"But I couldn't possibly put you to all that trouble."

"Please," I declared, "it's no trouble. I have almost a week before I fly home, with nothing to do, except visit a few libraries. Besides—it's such a lovely name: Saffron Orcas."

"Yes," she said. "Isn't it?"

We sat in silence for a while, until I noticed that she was shivering, and went down to my car and brought up a rug and put it around her shoulders. She drew away from it at first, glancing sharply up at me as though to question my intentions, but seeing that they were only to warm her, she relaxed, and snuggled into it gratefully. "Thank you," she said. "I'm sorry to be such a bother."

I assured her that she was no bother at all. "It's always coldest just before dawn," she said.

And after that, there seemed nothing more to say. The darkness weighed down upon us, separating us; huddled in the rug, she was a silhouette against the faint glimmer of starlight on a stone. I wondered what she was thinking, sitting there in silence; I wondered who she was, really—the niece of the Vicar of Saffron Orcas, wherever that was, or a girl from nowhere; what her childhood had been like—the nursery, the nanny, the school?—what young, fresh, child-faces of her youth were going through her mind in the dreamlike silence, in that dreamlike place. Or was she no girl at all, but herself a dream, left there by the past . . . a dream of long-dead Queens, of Elfrida and Eleanor, and Anne . . . of Nimue herself. . . ?

The night was turning gray around us; a few drops of dew seemed to fall from nowhere onto the stones. An absolute silence hung in the air; very gradually the stars paled, and in the east the sky turned ever so faintly luminous. A cock crowed far away, breaking the silence; it seemed to me that the past was going back into the past again, gray shapes fading into daylight . . . Merlin, Arthur, the ancient ones . . . slipping away from me, like fog into sunshine. A little breeze blew up from the southwest, and the first faint tint of rose appeared in the east, followed by a flush of palest gold, the rose and the gold deepening, growing brighter, climbing higher and higher toward a sky of opening blue . . . the whole wide midsummer day was climbing up from below the world's rim, rising steadily over Europe, over Hungary, over France, toward England, pushing the night away. . . .

The sun rose suddenly, directly over the small stone set in the trilithon, and bathed our faces in warm gold.

CHAPTER

2

From Salisbury we drove west through the Dorset
countryside with its meadows yellow with butter-
cups, its gentle hills crowned with copses of beech
and oak. The air was sweet with broom and fox-
glove, meadow-sweet and fool's parsley, and from
the hedges rose the scent of wild roses. The sky was
the high, far-off blue of English summer; and the
girl, with the guitar in her lap, and a little bundle
of her belongings, wrapped in a scarf, at her feet,
sang a little to herself or to an audience of birds:

> *It was Lord Caristoun's daughter*
> *That with young Alfred lay*
> *Alone by Indal water*

The Elixir

> *On that midsummer day.*
>
> *And there the Earl of Caristoun*
> *All with his armed bands*
> *Did find the fondling lovers*
> *Each in each other's hands.*
>
> *And he did slay young Alfred*
> *That was a Dorset man*
> *And carried to his castle*
> *His daughter Niniane.*
>
> *"A curse upon ye, father,*
> *If that indeed ye be,*
> *For ye have slain the fairest*
> *Of Dorset chivalry."*
>
> *Full seven years she dwelt there*
> *And prayed upon her knees*
> *That Caristoun's proud towers*
> *Would fall amongst the trees.*
>
> *They say by Indal water*
> *In Dorsetshire in June*
> *If two shall have met fair,*

Two more shall join them there:
Alfred and the Earl's daughter
With flowers in her hair.

And the trees climb on Caristoun.

The birds sang back to her, the sun shone, and I felt singularly lighthearted, considering that I hadn't slept at all. We had breakfasted in Salisbury on porridge, kippers, and tea, and ahead of us, somewhere, lay Saffron Orcas.

"The old ballads are so sad," I said. "As though young love was always doomed to die. Where did you find the song? It's a lovely tune."

"Yes," she agreed simply; "isn't it?

"I made it up last week."

I stared at her in surprise, and she looked back at me helplessly. "At least, I think I did," she said.

"It was just that it was there in my mind, as though it had always been."

She looked thoughtfully out at a long, quiet slope of meadow where a few cows grazed peacefully. "Is it always doomed, do you think?" she asked.

"Doomed?"

"Young love."

"As a matter of fact," I said, "I'm not at all sure that young people fall in love any more."

"What an extraordinary thing to say!" she exclaimed. "But then, you're an older man."

"Older men are also doomed," I said lightly. "In fact, we are all doomed, sooner or later."

"That's what the tree people say," she declared.

"Who are the tree people?"

But she shook her head. "I couldn't possibly explain," she said. "And anyway, I'd rather not talk about it."

And turning to her guitar again, she began to sing to herself.

> *Oh western wind, when wilt thou blow*
> *That the small rain down may rain?*
> *Christ, that my love were in my arms*
> *And I in my bed again.*

It all seemed so incongruous, the song and the slender, young, pale-gold and lily-white girl, that I burst out laughing. "I suppose you made that up, too," I said.

"I did not," she replied coldly. "That's from the

sixteenth century, and no one knows who made it up."

"I know," I said contritely. "And it's not 'may rain,' it's 'can rain.' I was testing you."

"Well, don't," she said. "It makes you sound like somebody's nanny."

"Obviously," I said, "that would never do. I'm not that old. Somebody's nanny indeed!"

"How old are you?" she asked. "Are you old enough to be my father?"

"Certainly not," I replied stiffly.

She gave a nod of satisfaction. "One never knows with Americans," she said.

Old? I felt curiously young, and not at all like a professor of history—on the contrary, much more the way I used to feel as an undergraduate on a Summer day in New Hampshire—full of spirit and wonderfully hopeful. Of what? I had no idea then, and I had none now.

I should have known, of course. When one is forty, and feels suddenly happy . . .

I was intensely aware of the girl; and yet, at the same time, I had no clear picture of her—that is, beyond her appearance, beyond the slender bones, the soft, golden hair, the delicately structured face —the eyes dreaming or suddenly alight, the white, arching throat, the sensitive hands folded on the guitar in her lap. I wondered who she was; a student, perhaps; a college girl on her Summer vacation? From Oxford, or Cambridge. . . ?

Whenever I glanced at her, she turned away, but I sensed that she was studying me. "Are you really an American?" she asked at last.

"Of course. Don't I seem one?"

"Actually, I'd have rather taken you for a colonial."

"A colonial?"

"Canada, perhaps. One thinks of an American as being . . . well . . . more like Mr. Hemingway perhaps. Or John Wayne."

I felt slightly confused; but whether it was because I disliked being taken for Hemingway or John Wayne—or because I didn't look enough like them—I wasn't sure. "After all," I said, "there are two hundred million of us."

She nodded. "That's what's so awful," she said.

"And some of us are black."

She sighed in a troubled way. "The Druids were small and dark," she said. "Merlin himself was tall, but he was quite thin. It was easy to stuff him into a tree, once you knew the proper spell."

"How do you know?" I asked lightly. "Were you there?"

"Funnily enough," she replied, smiling, "I'm not altogether sure."

I wanted—if only to get back at her for being taken for a colonial—to say: "I'd not have taken you for a witch." But I realized with a certain amusement that I really had no idea of what a witch in ancient Britain might have looked like; that is to say, when Britain was still a slow mixture of Aborigine, Minoan, Roman, and Celt, and before there were added the strains of Dane, Norwegian, Saxon, Angle, Jute, Norman, and Teuton. Out of that rich soil nourished by moisture from the Gulf Stream, and fed on tea from China and the Indies, bloomed the English long-stemmed rose now seated beside me in the rented Vauxhall.

At Shaftesbury, my being obliged to stop at a garage for petrol, Niniane asked me to excuse her while she attended to a few things. I watched the car for a time, and then, Niniane not returning, I decided to stroll about a bit among the small shops so different from those at home—the grocer, the butcher, the sweetshop from which Niniane herself suddenly emerged, looking, I thought, a little flushed. "There you are," she said; and seizing me by the hand, started smartly for the car. "Let's get on," she said; and marching straight ahead, with her chin in the air, murmured,

"Don't look back."

Had she had some unpleasant encounter? Or met someone she knew, and didn't want to see? I was mystified, but not for long. Ten miles out of Shaftesbury, she asked me to draw up at the edge of a meadow in the shade of a giant beech; and at once climbed out of the car, spread the rug on the ground, and motioned me to join her. Then, with a sigh of relief, and to my surprise, she drew out of the folds of her long skirt a small loaf of white bread, a small cheese, a can of sardines, a jar of gooseberry jam, and a bag of peppermints. "I couldn't reach the wine," she said, "but there's a stream at the foot of the meadow, and the water's quite good."

"I'd have taken you to lunch," I remonstrated. "You didn't have to buy all this."

"You paid for my breakfast," she said. "I can't let you do everything."

"Nonsense," I exclaimed, and reached for my wallet. "What did it all cost?"

She put out a restraining hand, light (I noticed) as a leaf. "I couldn't possibly let you," she declared. "It would be like stealing."

I thought that she turned a little pink. "You see," she admitted, "it didn't really cost me anything."

"You mean you . . . took . . . these things? The bread, the cheese?"

She nodded. "I suppose you could put it that way," she said. "But I shall pay for them, of course . . . Some day."

She gave me a candid look. "Besides," she explained, "they would have been given me, if I had asked. This is England, you know. People are very kind."

"But you didn't ask," I said.

She lifted her chin, and stared solemnly up at the sky. "I love peppermint drops," she declared. "My nanny always let me have some when I was good."

The curious part of it was that I wasn't really shocked, although I would have been, very much so, at home. Perhaps, for all I knew, people *were* kinder in England—though nothing in my reading had led me to think so. On the other hand, I found it hard to imagine anyone being anything but kind to Niniane.

Seated across from her in the shade of the great tree, with the green, gentle slope of the meadow below us, I had a chance to study her. She seemed very young, and both joyous and vulnerable at the same time . . . one of the flower generation, I thought. And indeed there was something almost flower-like about her, a brightness, a fragrance made visible. I tried to remember my own youth; had it ever been so delicate, so poised for flight? I couldn't be sure; it seemed somehow clodlike in comparison. She had a way of opening her eyes very wide, and they became full of light. When she smiled, it was like a child in pleasure, and her laugh was like a bubble floating in the air, purely free and joyous. She was young and lovely, and as remote as history; she could have stepped out of the past, she could have come from Astolat or Tintagel . . . except that the clothes she wore, the bright-colored blouse, the long woolen skirt, the sandal-like slippers of soft leather, all belonged to Carnaby Street rather than Camelot.

The meadow was at drowse with gnat-hum and

bee-drone, the air was Summer-sweet; a lark sang high in the air above us, trilling—halfway, it seemed, between a nightingale and a cricket. "When were you born?" she asked.

"In January."

"So was I! We're Capricorns."

"Splendid. And does that make us friends?"

"Naturally."

"That's good," I said. "Because I think you're a witch. Where have you hidden Arthur?"

"Arthur?"

"The Round Table, and all."

She laughed delightedly, and made believe to look through the folds of her skirt. "He isn't here," she said.

"And Merlin?"

"He isn't here, either."

"Perhaps you've hidden him in Saffron Orcas."

A cloud seemed suddenly to cross her face; all the fun drained out of it and for a moment she seemed much older. "It's time we were getting on," she said, and rose to her feet. "Come along, then."

She was quiet as we drove along, lost in some private world of her own, and—it seemed to me— uneasy in her thoughts. I wondered briefly if I had offended her, but a warm, shy smile reassured me;

whatever troubled her was apparently not of my doing.

It was late afternoon when we came to Sherborne with its castle; I would have liked to stop there, to visit the famous Abbey, now a school, and the ruins of Raleigh's Keep, but she demurred. "My cousin lives there," she said.

"But surely—in that case—"

"It was long ago," she said. "We haven't seen each other for years, not since we were children. He might not recognize me. And anyway, he's married."

It seemed odd, but I could see her point. A cousin of the Digbys wandering about the countryside with a guitar and a middle-aged stranger . . . an American, too. That is, if he *was* her cousin. I supposed I'd never know.

We left Sherborne with its Norman towers, with Raleigh's ruined Keep rising dimly among the trees behind us, and at Niniane's direction turned off the tarmac onto a country lane, which in turn gave way to another, and then to another. High hedges rose about us on either side, the home of countless flittering birds and climbing wild roses. Occasionally I caught sight of a farm, or a small hill, but I had little sense of where I was, or where I was going;

and it seemed to me, as we went on, that Niniane herself grew less and less certain, and more and more inclined to silence. Twilight was falling, the long, English twilight that goes on and on; the sun sank, but the sky still glowed in paler shades, lime-green, rose-pink . . .

"I think we go left at that signpost," she said at last, "but I'm not sure."

"We're lost, aren't we?" I remarked as cheer-fully as I could. The thought of spending a second sleepless night out of doors didn't appeal to me.

She didn't look at me. "I'm afraid so," she said.

"Tell me," I turned to face her. "Is there a Saffron Orcas? Or did you make it up last week?"

"Not last week," she said meekly. "Long ago. My cousin Peter and I."

"The one who lives in the castle?"

She nodded her head. She still wouldn't look at me.

"I see. So we're really going nowhere at all."

"I'm terribly sorry," she said. "It seemed such fun, somehow—last night, that is, and then this morning. And I did have to be from somewhere.

"Are you very angry with me?"

"I'm not angry at all," I said; and it was the truth. I was more amused than angry, and more bewildered than anything else. "We'd best go back to Sherborne," I said. "And I shall hand you over to your cousin—guitar and all."

At that, she turned to face me, eyes wide with dismay. "No, please," she said in a little-girl voice; "don't do that." She kept on staring at me, but I could see that she was thinking very hard. "There's quite a nice inn near here," she said at last, "and I do know the way to it."

"Well," I began uncertainly.

"It's called the Dog and Duck. That's the turn, I think, just on ahead."

She laid her narrow, light hand on mine for a moment; it felt like the fall of a rose petal. "I'm so terribly tired," she said. "I do need the sleep."

She gave a little sigh. "We could sleep under a hedge," she said, "but a bed is much nicer. Besides, there are the tree people; and we have only one rug between us. I might have to marry you, and you wouldn't like that at all."

"Who on earth are the tree people?" I asked.

But she didn't answer; and we turned down the lane at the sign.

CHAPTER

3

"Niniane," I said.

We were dining on a rabbit pie in the small dining room off the public bar at the Dog and Duck. We'd been given two rooms—the only rooms, I was told, in the old inn whose carved oak-paneled walls, dark with age, returned the lamplight like candles reflected in a pool. "I can't keep calling you Niniane," I said. "It's a name right out of Malory. It makes me feel silly."

"The girls at school used to call me Ninny," she said, "but I never liked it much. Peter called me Anna."

"Ah," I said. "The cousin again."

"Well," she said judiciously, "you could call me Anne."

Yes, I thought, I should like that. Anne. "And what will you call me?" I asked.

"I shall call you by your name, I expect," she said. "Mr. Irwin. Mr. Robert Irwin. It is Robert— isn't it?"

"Yes. But I've never liked it."

"Then I shall make up a name for you. Gareth? Gawaine?"

"We're still in Malory," I said.

"Finmole?"

"Now you've gone Irish," I said.

She sighed. "He was Cuchulainn's son," she said. "Shall I go Welsh?"

"Irwin," she said. "Euwen. Mr. Euwen Irwin."

And smiling her warm smile at me, she added, "Of Boston, America."

"I'm not from Boston," I said. "Whatever made you think so?"

"You said New England . . ."

"New England is larger than all your counties put together."

"Oh," she said.

At least, I thought, Oxford or no, she's never

studied geography. "I hope you realize," I remarked, "that none of our conversation so far has
made any sense at all."

"I know," she said. "Isn't it lovely?"

"Look," I said, "if we're going to be non-
sensical . . ."

"Oh, but we're not," she exclaimed. "Not really.
Actually, we're being very sensible. Because we
don't know each other at all, you see—and don't
even know if we want to, really. At least—"

She hesitated, and then plunged on. "At least,
you don't. Do you?"

It was less a question than a statement, and I
paused to think about it. I had never been what
one might call adventurous; I had always gone
slowly into such intimacies as I had known. And
yet. . . . Perhaps it was the very strangeness of my
situation—the long, slow evening folding about us,
the inn, the picnic by the meadow . . . being so
far from home . . .

"I think I do," I said.

Her long slim finger made patterns on the
checkered tablecloth between us. "I didn't expect
you to say that," she said slowly. "In that case . . ."

She gave me a troubled smile. "I suppose I

shall have to think about it too," she said.

But she was tired; the skin under her eyes showed a faint bluish tinge. "I'm sleepy, Euwen," she said.

I was tired, too; I felt a little light-headed. "My name isn't Euwen," I said, "and it's been a lovely day."

"Heavenly," she agreed. "But I shall fall asleep any moment."

I waited outside the door of her room while she lighted the lamp at her bedside, and pulled the shutters together. "Against the tree people," she said; and "Thank you for everything."

In my own room the moonlight had laid a milk-white diagonal across the black oak floor, and everything else was in darkness. I went to the window and looked out at the moon-flooded night, at the spidery branches of the trees, the black, velvet shadows, the dim fields rolling away toward a moon-misty horizon. I breathed in the damp, earth-sweet night air.

I stood a long time staring out at the night, listening in the stillness to the sound of long-dead battle horns, to the wild, bittersweet, silent piping

of the clans. And again, as at Stonehenge, I had a
feeling that the past was all around me, that there,
in the moon-misted fields, Richard hunted with his
Barons, and Titania slept and dreamed. And that
Anne was part of it, and that I was part of it.

A cloud covered the moon, and distant thunder
rumbled in the west. I turned from the window at
last, and went to bed, and slept.

And dreamed. I dreamed that I was in a familiar
wood—which was all the more strange because it
was unlike any wood that I had ever seen. It was a
very old wood, almost primeval; and it had its own
life, its own being, which surrounded me with love
and terror. Strange, unclean creatures lurked there,
appearing for a moment, scarcely seen through the
underbrush, and vanished again. They were somehow obscene, and I feared them, but the trees shel-
tered me, threw their strong, leaf-soft limbs around
me, their curiously soft, sheltering limbs. . . .

I woke with Anne in my bed, her head buried
against my breast, her arms wound tight around
me. A storm was rumbling overhead; a moment
later a burst of lightning blazed through the room,
and thunder crashed directly above us. Anne gave

a moan, and her whole body went taut. "Make them stop!" she whispered. "Oh—make them stop!"

Her hair was like silk against my cheek. "It's all right," I said. "It's all right."

"I'm frightened," she said.

I suppose I would have been too, if I had been alone. "It's only a storm," I said. At least it was real; it was better than those obscene creatures in the wood.

The storm seemed to be passing; I could hear the rain outside, and on the roof; the worst of it was over. Anne stirred, and sighed. "I'm sorry," she said. "I'll go now." But a last peal of thunder shook the room, and she turned back to me in a panic. I tightened my arms around her.

She didn't say anything. Slowly, ever so slowly, she lifted her face to mine, and, bending, I kissed her.

Her mouth was incredibly soft . . . berry-soft, flower-soft, mouse-soft. And her body, under the simple shift she wore, was . . . how can I describe it? It was all of April poured into a single leaf; rain-soft and sun-ripened, cool as a petal but bursting with bloom . . . mothlike, stirring, quivering, un-folding . . . enfolding . . .

I wanted to plunge into that softness, to lose myself in it, to stay in that softness forever.

It was only afterwards that it occurred to me to wonder at her excellence. I was obviously not her first lover; but even so, I would have expected a little awkwardness, a lack of ease, of grace—but there was none, only a lovely harmonious flow, an ever-rising flow of joy, coming at last to a great cry of rapture—or was it anguish?—And then a slow subsiding into peace.

We lay together, clasped in each other's arms, joined in a common moisture, until she slowly drew back and lay apart from me, one arm upraised, the elbow bent, her hand behind her head, the other lying at her side, the palm of her hand upturned. The storm had passed, and little glimmers of cloud-light showed pale at the windows. I realized, only then, that I hadn't closed the shutters, and glanced at her anxiously, but she didn't seem to have noticed.

I heard her give a little sigh. "I shouldn't have done that, really," she said. "But it was lovely." She turned toward me, suddenly worried. "You don't hate me, Euwen?" she asked.

It astonished me. "Hate you? It's all the other

way. I . . ." I wanted to say "I love you," but it sounded too easy, too glib; and besides, was it true? "It made me very happy," I said.

"But—" I took a deep breath—"Why always Euwen? Was he. . . ? that is. . . . After all . . ."

Her little bubble of laughter floated toward the ceiling. "He wasn't anybody, really," she said. "Actually, he was a friend of Rupert Brooke." Her voice took on a note of conviction. "He used to come to tea at Grantchester," she said. "Tea, with strawberry jam."

In 1912?, I thought.

"You didn't close the shutters," she said suddenly, out of nowhere.

"No, I didn't. . . . Anne; how old are you?"

"How old do you think?"

"Twenty?"

Again the bubble laugh. "Oh," she said, "thank you for that!" And then, seriously,

"I'm older than I seem."

"Thirty?"

She turned back to me, and put her head down on my breast. "Don't go on," she said. "There are all kinds of things it's better not to know. Because then you can believe what you want to believe."

"Like Saffron Orcas?"

She seemed to burrow deeper into my side. "I know," she said in a muffled voice. "It was all so real to me, for so long, that I suppose I thought it might be there after all. Only it wasn't. I hated it not being there; it makes me feel sad, as though my childhood wasn't there, either. As though I'd lost the child that was me."

She pushed herself away, and sat up, a pale, dimly seen figure beside me. "It was your fault," she said fiercely. "You should never have said you'd take me there."

She sighed heavily, and let herself down beside me again. "But you did bring me to the Dog and Duck," she said. "And it was lovely."

Her body was cool in my arms, and smooth as cream. "You never knew Rupert Brooke," I said. "And it wasn't tea with strawberry jam, it was honey. 'Stands the Church clock at ten-to-three? And is there honey still for tea?'"

"He was a friend of my cousin Peter," she said slowly, "and I was in love with him. For quite a long while. As a matter of fact . . ."

"Of course," I said; and, smiling, stopped her mouth with a kiss.

It was bright morning when we woke. I lay propped up on my elbow, gazing at her, marveling. The closed, blue-shadowed eyes, the full, half-smiling mouth, the young, delicate face, the long, slender neck . . . pale golden hair spread like a fan across the pillow, marble-round, flower-white arms and shoulders, like some painting or statue of long ago, from the Renaissance, from ancient Greece. . . .

Perhaps, I thought, she had known Brooke, after all. And Shelley, and Lovelace, and Donne, and Spenser. Or if not this very girl, then someone exactly like her.

And before Spenser; Malory himself, even. And Merlin.

"Nimue," I said softly. "Niniane."

She opened her eyes, blue as the morning, and stared at me in a puzzled way. Then, suddenly, she remembered, and turned away. "You hate me," she said.

I was dumbfounded. "Good God!" I cried. "Why should I hate you?"

"My nanny always said I was too bold," she declared. "She used to tell me I was shameless. And

I have been shameless, haven't I? I was afraid you'd hate me for it."

She turned back slowly, and looked at me. "I always thought one was supposed to, afterwards," she said. "And sometimes I have. But I don't now . . . for some reason."

She gave me a timid smile. "Is that dreadful?" she asked. "I mean . . . does that trouble you? Because I don't want to—"

"I love you," I said. At least, I meant to say it, but I think I shouted it.

The effect on Anne was surprising. She flushed, and her eyes suddenly filled with tears. "You didn't have to say that," she said. "But it was dear of you."

To tell the truth, I was as astonished as she was, but in full tide, swept along beyond accounting, touched to the heart by that combination of beauty and humility which seemed somehow piteous and awesome all at once; as though one had found a goddess—or a child—in tears, and felt the need to worship and comfort at the same time. "I know I didn't have to," I said; "but I do."

She sat, the sheet drawn up about her, gravely

regarding me. "What am I going to do with you?" she asked at last.

"I don't know. Love me, I hope."

"Yes," she said slowly. "Perhaps. I think so. But for how long?"

"At least until tomorrow," I exclaimed. "Or—" in a moment of inspiration—"until we get to Saffron Orcas."

She smiled at that, and held her hand out to me. "You know," she said, "you're rather a dear. Shall we really find it, Robert-Euwen?"

"Yes," I said. And at that moment, with the sun pouring in the window, turning everything to gold, I really thought we might.

"Of course," I said.

She must have believed me, for she sat for a moment or two with her head thrown back, smiling a little. But then, abruptly, her mood changed, her head drooped, and she looked uncertain again. "You haven't had your tea yet," she said forlornly. "You might feel quite differently after."

She was right, in a way. We sat out in the little courtyard of the inn, in the bright sunshine, holding each other's hands, and eating our breakfast—of scones and jam and chocolate—more and more slowly. Pigeons preened and fluttered over the cobbled stones at our feet, and wasps buzzed around us. "The thing is," I said miserably, "I've got to be getting home again."

"Oh," she said, and slowly let go of my hand. "I see," she said.

"You don't see at all," I told her. "I don't want to go. It's only that my classes start—"

"In July?"

"It's the Summer session, and I've signed up for it."

"Of course," she said. "Well . . ."

"I do love you," I exclaimed desperately.

She looked at me gravely for a long moment, and her expression softened. "Yes," she said; "perhaps you do." And reaching over, she took my hand again. "How long have we?" she asked.

"Today is—what? Tuesday?"

"Wednesday. Woden's Day."

"My plane leaves on Sunday."

"Four days," she said. She took a deep breath. "There's a lovely old inn near Boscastle," she said thoughtfully, "near Tintagel Head."

CHAPTER

4

We were sitting in the garden of the Sword and Crown, looking out at the western ocean whose waters sucked at the shingle far below. The Cornish cliffs stood up around us, gray and brown, with the sea all flat and silver in the sun, and small, so far away. Distant, in the east, the ruined walls of Tintagel loomed on their rock above the water; all was still, except for the steady flow of air from the west, the swift, high passage of clouds up from the Gulf Stream, the occasional harsh cry of a seabird.

We had been two days at the inn, two wholly happy days. We had walked along the cliffs from which, long ago, messengers had seen the Phoeni-

cian galleys beating up from the south in search of
Cornish tin; we had climbed down through the
bracken to the shingle, and there bathed in the
clear green waters of the Atlantic. And always, in
the distance, there was Tintagel, sometimes veiled
in mist, or darkened by cloud shadows. Tintagel—
where Arthur was born, they said, either of Uther
or Gorlois . . . Arthur of the Round Table, Guinevere's husband, Lancelot's friend.

"The myth," I said, "or the reality. Which do you
choose?"

"The myth, of course," said Anne. "Because it's
closer to the truth."

"Or to the dream," I said. "Arthur, in full
armor, astride a battle-charger, surrounded by his
knights . . ."

"That's how it was," she said stubbornly. "Not
in reality, perhaps—but in truth."

"In reality," I said, "he wore a bit of chain mail
over leather, and his horse was a half-wild Shetland.
And his knights were farmers."

"Not Lancelot," she said.

"Lancelot came from France. He was altogether
Gallic."

"Of course," she said. "No proper Englishman

would ever dream of taking his sovereign's wife to bed."

"But Guinevere was herself from across the Channel . . ."

"Arthur should have wed closer to home," she declared. "He should have married Morven, the Duke of Cornwall's daughter."

I pointed out that after all, most of the Arthurian cycle had had its roots in France.

She looked over at the old castle on its rock, misty in the distance. "That didn't come from France," she said. "What's more, Gawaine was an Irishman.

"Not a Firbolg, mind you," she added. "A Celt."

I saw her suddenly as a delicious little morsel of English pride, and I burst out laughing. "I love you," I said. "Even though you talk a lot of nonsense."

She bent her head, and studied her long, slender fingers. When she spoke, it was with great earnestness.

"It isn't nonsense, Robbie-Euwen," she said. "It's at the heart of everything. Do you know man's main advantage over the other animals?"

"He has a thumb," I said.

"No," said Anne. "He has fairy tales."

"He also has a history."

"Everything has a history, Robbie; even the rocks. But man has legends and dreams, and they weave one into another, and he is part of them, and they are part of him. The trees have history, but they have no legends."

"The oak," I said, "might remember that it was Thor's sacred tree until Saint Boniface took an ax to it in 723."

She gave me a sudden, startled look. "Perhaps that explains it," she said. "He was an ancestor of mine, you see. Winfrid, later Boniface. I'd forgotten all that about the oak. That's why the tree people . . ."

"Anne," I said severely, "have you ever actually seen these tree people?"

"No," she admitted. "But I've heard them. First there's a whispering, and then a rustling, and then a scurrying, and then a yattering. They yatter at me."

"What do they say?"

She shrugged her shoulders helplessly. "I've no idea," she said. "It's just frightening, that's all. Don't let's talk about it."

"Very well. What shall we talk about?"

"You and me."

Yes, I thought; you and me. But one cannot talk one's way into—or out of—an enchantment; it lay there in the air, iridescent, light . . . I must keep it there, I said to myself. I reminded myself that it had no past, and no foreseeable future; I told myself that to the young today love is little more than a soap bubble; one took a lover for a night, or a week, for convenience, or out of apathy or hunger. At least, I had been told so, in all the books and magazines.

So I simply smiled at her; and she smiled back at me.

At another time, she said:

"The world is really rather horrid, Euwen. And I'm rather horrid, too."

"All young people think the world is horrid," I said, "and always have. That is why they want to change it. The world is no worse than the people in it. By the time young people learn this, they have grown old."

"Then you don't believe there is such a thing as abstract evil?"

"There is darkness," I said, "and light."

"Darkness was all around us once," she said

slowly. "In the deep forests, in the great swamps. It was against that darkness that Arthur fought—and Merlin, too, until he was too old."

"Until he lost his head over a girl," I said.

"Until he was too old," she repeated stubbornly. She seemed to blaze at me for a moment; then, in a sudden change of mood, she clapped her hands and laughed delightedly. "We've had our first quarrel," she exclaimed. "Isn't it fun?"

But if there was delight in our days—at looking at each other across a table or a room, falling into each other's eyes and drowning there—at seeing her in the sun, dreamy and content, or merry; the wonder of watching her running across a meadow in the wind, as light as thistledown, or poised as though for flight at the cliff's edge while the sunlight made a halo of her golden hair—there was even more enchantment at night when we lay together, lost in a dream, while the sea whispered and foamed on the rocks below. Or, from the window, watched the golden glimmer of the moon on the black water, and thought of Tristan and Ysolt, of lovers dead and gone . . .

Long gone, the two that here did lie [she sang]
'Ere Ethelbert had sat his throne.

The Elixir

Long gone, long gone.
Long gone, the kiss of heart and tongue,
And Eleanore in her beautie,
Long gone, long gone.
All loving hearts that here did play,
Long gone. The Lady Anne Boleyn
That Henry set a crown upon,
Long gone. Long gone away.

"Actually," she said, "there were two Ysolts; the Irish girl, and Yseult of the White Hands, who was daughter to the King of Brittany. Tristan left the Irish girl for the other, and came to no good end. He was an uncertain hero, given to moods; I could have told him."

"Of course," I said, nuzzling her neck which was soft and supple as a swan's. "But you didn't, did you?"

She lay quiet in my arms for a moment, and then pushed me away. "I only said I could have," she declared.

After we had made love, she liked to lie with her head on my breast, and my arms around her; after a while she would rouse herself, and turn away from me, and fall asleep with her cheek on her hand, like a child. There was always something of the child about her, something that touched me deeply. The very first night at the inn, I slipped out of bed to attend to something, and in her sleep she put out her hand to feel for me beside her. But the bed was empty; her hand first explored gently, then more urgently, and finally swept about desperately; convinced of betrayal at last, she gave an angry flounce, drew the sheet over her head, and announced clearly but with resignation: "He has run away somewhere." When I got back into bed again, she was still sound asleep, but she gave a little sigh as though of relief.

Not all her songs were sad. In the bright morning, on the other side of the lavatory door, I could hear her singing "Land of Hope and Glory." She told me afterwards that she had been cutting her toenails. "I always sing 'Land of Hope and Glory' when cutting my toenails," she declared.

It was on the following day, Thor's Day, that Anne asked to be taken to Camelford; she had in mind, she said, a visit to the apothecary. We found his shop in a very old house indeed, tucked away in a narrow lane beneath the branches of an ancient oak, and all but overrun with ivy. I left Anne off, and went on to visit the local bookshop in search of whatever I could find: a Nennius's *Historia Britonum* (1838) or even a Layamon *Brut* edited by Sir Francis Meader in 1847. It was not very likely; but the bookshop did produce a copy of Zimmer's *Nennius Vindicatus* (1893).

Mr. Jones, the proprietor, a tall, thin, puckish-looking man, with a wide gash of mouth which he kept tightly folded, a crab-apple face, and gray eyes that stared at me without blinking, stroked the worn binding of the book with long, spatulate fingers. "I take it, sir," he said, "that you are a student of our history. How very nice. As you no doubt know, our little town was once the site of Camelot. King Arthur's Camelot, of course. You knew that?"

"Yes," I said. "Though some scholars place it at Caerleon, and some at Cadbury, and others at Winchester of Queen's Camel, in Somersetshire."

Mr. Jones's face turned a faint shade of pink. "Not at all!" he exclaimed; "not at all. It was Geoffrey of Monmouth who claimed Camelot for Caerleon, in his own county of Monmouth; and as for Queen's Camel, I am assured by none other than Dr. John Weaver, the eminent zoologist, that the beast in question was, actually, an animal brought over from Arabia by one Arafat.

"What is more," he went on, his voice trembling a little with suppressed feeling, "there is the evidence of Tintagel, which lies within a few hours' ride of us; that is, of course, by horse; Arthur did not have a motor car."

He was completely serious. "No," I said; "no, he did not. But would he have built his castle so close to the one in which he was born?"

"Ah," said Mr. Jones; "a nice point, a nice point. He would have done, do you see; feeling himself at home, as it were. However, you have the historian's view. Quite right. Quite right."

"I am an historian," I said.

"Oh," said Mr. Jones. "How very nice. From where, may I ask? I am not familiar with your accent."

"I am an American."

"Are you really? An American! Well, well, indeed . . . an American historian. You haven't had very much history yourselves, have you?"

"Not very much," I agreed.

"As a matter of fact," said Mr. Jones, "I have a book by a countryman of yours; a Mr. Feis, I believe it won a prize of some sort. I haven't read it myself, but I understand that it is about the war. Would you care to see it?"

"No thank you," I said. "I happen to have all of Professor Feis's books at home. I shall just take the Zimmer."

"That will be thirteen shillings and sixpence," said Mr. Jones. "Come in again. Would you care to have me cast about for a Nennius or a Layamon for you?"

"I shall be going home within a week," I said.

"Too bad that," said Mr. Jones. "There's a good bit of history hereabouts. However—"

"There's too much of it," I said.

"Yes," said Mr. Jones vaguely; "I dare say. No doubt you'll be more comfortable with less."

Mr. Jones placed the book in a brown paper bag, I paid him the 13s 6d, and went out into the sunshine in search of Anne.

She was not in the apothecary's; in fact, no one seemed to be there at all. The door being locked, I peered in through the window, and saw nothing but a stuffed owl on top of a glass case, in which I could distinguish a number of bottles and jars of different colors.

I was turning away in uncertainty, wondering
what to do, when, in the shadows behind the great
oak I caught sight of Anne herself coming toward
me. Whether it was from having been in bright sunlight, and looking into deep leaf-shadow, or for
some other reason, a trick of light, perhaps, I saw
her for a moment—and no more than a moment—in
a high-bodiced, long green kirtle such as women
wore in the Middle Ages; she was carrying a small
bunch of flowers in one hand, while the other, held
high, seemed to serve as a perch for a large bird,
a raven or a hawk. From the poise of her upturned
head, already so familiar to me, I would have said
that she was talking to it. The entire vision, which
lasted for no more than three or four seconds, reminded me of one of those Gothic tapestries which
depict a hunting scene of long ago, with pages,
foresters and dogs, and a lady with a merlin on her
wrist. . . .

The vision, as I say, lasted only a moment; and
then Anne was coming through the leaf-dapple
dressed in her familiar skirt and blouse, smiling
and holding a small bunch of flowers in her hand.
But of a hawk, or any bird, there was no sign.

"There you are," she said contentedly. "You

were so long, I thought I'd lost you. What is in the bag? Is it something good to eat?"

"It's a book," I said shortly.

At my tone, the light died out on her face, and she peered at me anxiously. "You're not angry?" she asked. "I only went a short way in the wood."

As a matter of fact, I wasn't angry; I was somewhat shaken, and more than a little perplexed. I do not ordinarily see visions. And the more I thought about it, the more I began to wonder if the owl in the apothecary's had really been stuffed after all. As I recalled, he had seemed to glare at me with singularly yellow eyes.

"Angry?" I said. "Of course not."

She appeared relieved, and linked her arm happily in mine. "I did hope you'd something good in the bag," she said as we started toward the car, "because it's high time we had our tea."

CHAPTER

5

The last days went by all too quickly, and it was time for me to return to the States. Some memories of those few days are unusually bright: I remember, for instance, a lunch we had at the Red Lion Inn at Clovelly on its rock above the sea, the little, gabled houses climbing one on top of the other along the steep, cobbled street, and the blue water shining beneath us in the sun. It was at Clovelly that Anne talked a little about her childhood; but whether it was indeed her own childhood, or someone else's—or even, perhaps, something she had made up—I didn't know.

Not that I cared very much. Whoever she was, I loved her; but there was no future in it, and I knew it. She could no more have settled down in a small New England college town as the wife of a professor of history, than I could . . . fly. "I shall be flying home," I said, "in two days' time."

"I know," she said. "I wish it weren't so. I have a thing about flying."

I admitted that I didn't really enjoy it. "But it saves time," I declared.

She shrugged her shoulders. "Of course," she said, "if you could save a lot of time; if you could save centuries. . . ." Her face took on a curious inward look. "If you could land—" she began, and then broke off abruptly. "Where do you land, by the way?" she asked.

"In New York. And after that, in Boston."

"We shall be six hours apart," she said. "It will be . . . When do you leave?"

"At nine at night."

"And you'll arrive in New York at"—she counted on her fingers—"eleven. But here it will be four o'clock in the morning. And I shall miss you very much."

She gazed out somberly over the water, silent and silver below us. High in the sky a jet was knifing in from the west; it would be moments before the muted thunder of its passage could reach us. She seemed far off, her thoughts somewhere distant.

"I ran away once," she said; "when I was little. I went to look for fairies."

She smiled; but not at me. It was as though she were smiling at something long ago. "There was a tiny woody island in a stream that ran through the meadow where we lived," she said. "I had a little friend named Francesca who lived next door. One morning I got up terribly early, before the sun was up, and I put on my mother's opera cloak over my nightie, and I climbed out of the window, and Francesca came out, and we went to the woody island to look for fairies. Everything was wet with dew, and we walked through the fields in our long, draggled nighties. I expect we were eight, or thereabouts. A milkman came along in his cart, and when he saw us, he said 'Cor, blimey.' When we got to the island, we picked flowers and made wreaths of them, and Francesca fell asleep. But I looked for fairies, and I found lots of them; they were very small, and mostly in dewdrops and cowslips and under little stones. After a while I climbed up into a tree and I sat there. Of course, they'd discovered the open windows at home, and everyone was frantic; my nanny sent for the police constable, and Francesca's mother sent for the Boy Scouts. So after a while, I saw the constable coming across the meadow, and I came down from the tree because I was afraid the Boy Scouts would climb the tree after me. So they took us home, and Francesca cried and cried, and was forgiven, and treated like a heroine. It was most unfair. She was given a kitten, and I was sent to bed without any breakfast— or any lunch or tea, either. And I got an awful caning from my father, who didn't believe about the fairies at all."

"Your father," I said slowly. "I thought you lived with your uncle?"

"Oh," she said, and after a pause: "that was another time. Anyway, my father didn't believe me. But funnily enough, my godfather did; he got very excited, and asked me all kinds of questions. About the fairies, and all."

"And who," I asked, smiling at her still-childish eagerness, "was your godfather?"

"Edmund Spenser," she said.

It was a charming story: the two little girls in their long trailing nightdresses walking barefoot through the dew-drenched grass. And of course there could be any number of people in England named Spenser. If she had made it all up, she could have found an even more unlikely godfather: the rector of Ightham, for instance, or the Archbishop of Canterbury. Or even Sir Arthur Conan Doyle.

She was looking at me brightly but a little anxiously. "What are you thinking?" she asked; "sitting there with such a solemn face?"

I replied ruefully that I was thinking that in the few days we had been together, she had managed thoroughly to confuse me.

She laughed delightedly. "Rule Britannia!" she exclaimed.

Then there was the afternoon I found her seated on a low stone wall by the roadside, singing to a group of young people, and accompanying herself as usual on the guitar. Her audience sat straggled on the grass, the young men bearded, with long, bushy hair, the women in worn Levis or ankle-length gowns strung with beads and ornaments, or wreathed with flowers. They were wander-birds, on their way from here to there; they carried their

The Elixir

belongings in a pack or bundled in a scarf at the end of a stick.

Anne was singing an old song: in her pure, young voice, she sang:

> *Weep no more, sad fountains;*
> *What need you flow so fast?*
> *Look how the snowy mountains*
> *Heaven's sun doth gently waste.*
> *But my Sun's heavenly eyes*
> *View not your weeping,*
> *That now lies sleeping*
> *Softly,*
> > *now softly lies*
> *Sleeping.*

At the end, she sat for a moment, her head tilted upward in the way she had, as though listening; then, smiling gently, she launched into a Restoration ballad:

> *When I came down from Fetheringstone,*
> *There came three damsels down with me:*
> *One by the name of Faith, and one*
> *Was Hope, and one was Charity.*

And when I came from Winchelsea
My middle years were just begun,
And my three damsels were with me
As they had done in Fetheringstone.
But when I came from Ravenglass
That stands beside the Irish sea,
I'd lost my best and youngest lass,
And had but Hope and Charity.
And now I'm old and all bereft,
And many a mile from Fetheringstone
And I shall live on what is left,
Old wrinkled Charity alone.

It was a peaceful scene, bathed in the warm glow of summer: the green meadow, the golden light, the young people in their colorful tatters, all seemed somehow medieval, to belong to an earlier time. And I could see that Anne was happy.

But later that evening in the early twilight, as the sound of bells came drifting across the fields and across the hills, she wept. "They always make me cry," she said; "the church bells of England. They sound so lonely; and they come from so far away."

I held her and comforted her as best I could.

And that night we clung together more desperately than ever. "I'm growing old," she cried. "It's all going by so fast!" And later, in her sleep, I thought I heard her murmur,

"Bedivere."

In the morning, in the lavatory, I heard her singing "Land of Hope and Glory."

We made an early start, for she wanted me to let her off in Bath, where she said she had an aunt; and because she preferred not to have to say good-bye to me in the noise and bustle of an airport. And to tell the truth, it suited me very well; I thought the drive from Bath to London, across Wiltshire, Hampshire, and Surrey, would bring me back to myself again, to a more reasonable state of mind. I had had a love affair with a stranger; it was bewildering; it was enchanting, but it was over. I had my lectures to think of; on the plane I must begin to assemble my notes.

The west coast, by Clovelly and Porlock, would have been a prettier drive, but it would have taken too long. We went north, by Princetown, over the great bleak moor itself, swept bare by the winds; the swift-moving clouds sent shadows rippling across the tors and the bogs with their scatters of gorse and bracken. All was silence, the true silence, older than Camelot, older than Tintagel.

We, too, said little on the long drive across the moor. In that motionless arc of earth and sky, the years seemed to weigh nothing, I carried them like a feather: my youth, my age, the past, the future, all lay within that same bowl of air, that flow of space from horizon to horizon, no more distant from one another than Lydford and Bridestowe.

A strange euphoria! I should have been unhappy, but I was not. Anne sat as she had that very first day, on the way from Salisbury, the guitar in her lap; now and then she reached out to touch me, and her warm hand curled itself in mine. Our time to-gether was nearly at an end; we were about to part, never, in all likelihood, to see each other again. I had no way to reach her, no address; even the name she had given me, "Mellers," was probably false. And yet, for some reason, I felt at peace. As though there was all the time in the world.

We came down into Devonshire with its richer, redder earth, and on up into the rolling, cloud-banked hills of Somerset with their gold and green patchwork fields of mustard, wheat and barley. And so, finally, to Bath with its great houses. There, among the black Georgian pillars of Stall Street, Anne bade me stop, and with a long, last, smiling look, bent to kiss me. "Goodbye, Euwen," she said. "Have a good flight." And as she turned away—

"May the road rise before you. Go n'eiri do bhothar leat."

She hesitated a moment. "Don't trust the tree people," she said.

And she was gone. I drove slowly down the street, willing myself not to look back; but as I turned a corner I thought I saw her for a moment; she was entering the Pump Room, leaning on the arm of a Regency dandy complete with the high, conical hat, the many-caped long coat, the black, shining Hessians. She was laughing up at him, and her golden hair was piled in curls on top of her head. She was wearing a long, high-breasted gown, and she carried a large, broad-brimmed hat in her hand instead of the guitar, but there was no mistaking the pose—the uptilted head, the long, slim throat, the delicate features.

Except that, of course, it couldn't have been.

Just the same, I turned and went back. The Pump Room was empty, except for two old gentle-

men in their chairs, both of whom regarded me
with disfavor.

"Did," I asked politely, "a young lady come in
here with her escort a few minutes ago?"

It took them a moment or two to answer, during
which they stared at me as though I were some
sort of strange animal. At last one of the old gentle-
men cleared his throat.

"Scarcely," he said.

"Quite," said the other.

I went out and got into my car and started for
London. There was too much history in England,
too many voices of the past. Even the two old men
in their chairs—now that I thought of it—had had
a gray and ghostly look.

I drove very fast; I wanted to be away from
there. I longed for the clear, empty air of Massachusetts, for the simple history of the New
World. . . .

The Treaty of Ghent was signed on Decem-
ber 24, 1814. Geronimo, Chief of the Chiricahua
Apaches, surrendered in March, 1886.

The last witch was hanged in Salem in 1693.

I was halfway across Wiltshire when it occurred

to me that some motion picture company might have been making a film in Bath. I was in Hampshire before I remembered that I hadn't seen any of the paraphernalia of picture making—no cameras, lights, director, crew. . . .

It wasn't the tree people I needed to be afraid of, I told myself; it was my own imagination.

It was late when I got to Heathrow, and I was very tired; and by the time I had turned my car in to the rental people, and gone through the baggage and passenger check, all I wanted to do was sleep. It seemed to me that there was an unusual amount of confusion at the airport. I went on board the BOAC jet, and sank down into my seat, and closed my eyes. When I opened them, we were already lifting off the runway, headed for home.

I found myself seated between a large, elderly English lady, and a very black gentleman from the United States. On the lady's lap was a copy of the *Daily Mail*—the first newspaper I had seen in a week. And the headline brought me up with a shock.

"British Jet Hijacked By Guerrillas."

Not only a BOAC jet, apparently, but two others —a TWA from the United States and a Swissair from Basle—had been commandeered at gunpoint by Arab commandos, and taken to an improvised landing strip in the Jordan desert north of Amman. There some three hundred passengers were being held hostage, the planes—and their passengers—to be blown up in three days unless Arab demands against Israel were met.

"Ridiculous," said the English lady. "Absolute rubbish."

And she added firmly,

"It's high time something were done."

"Ah," said the black gentleman on the other side of me. "But it is very difficult for an elephant to crush a gnat."

"I suppose," said the lady, "that by 'elephant' you mean the United States of America, since we are not quite as large as we were. However, we've no need. We should send in Simon Lovat, with a few good people. And we will, too, before we're done. Mark my words."

"I'm sure," I said sleepily, "that President Nixon . . ."

I got no further. "Rubbish!" she exclaimed. You're afraid of the Soviets, that's the truth of it. And no wonder—since the Russians are not at all afraid to lie and cheat like billy-o, and you are. You're idealists, you know; and that's your trouble."

I found that I had great difficulty keeping my eyes open. "At least we're trying . . ." I mumbled.

"Nonsense," said the lady. "Truth is, people haven't changed in heaven knows how long. We're down at the moment, we British, but we'll be up again. Mark my words: they won't dare blow up a British airliner. A TWA, perhaps, or the Swiss one; but not ours. We'll send Allenby . . . Kitchener . . ."

"He was too late at Khartoum," said the black politely.

She gave a snort. "Wolseley's fault," she said. "But we got there just the same. And we taught the Mahdi a lesson, too."

I was asleep, of course. When I awoke, it was pitch black, and the plane was coming to what seemed like an unusually bumpy stop. I looked out the window for the lights of Kennedy International, but there was only darkness, though a few torches seemed to be moving about at some distance from us. I could vaguely make out the loom of what appeared to be a large aircraft nearby. "Where are we?" I asked.

A harsh voice with a guttural accent answered me. "You are at Ga Khanna," it said; "and you have just three minutes to get out of the plane before we blow it up."

_____

6

I found myself on the desert floor, along with some three or four hundred other hostages—or captives, for that was what we were. I was aware, mostly, of tremendous confusion, shouts and cries of Arab hijackers, wailing of infants, and the fright and indignation of women. And I was aware, too, of the intense cold, and the desert smell, dusty, sweet and mingled with the odor of gasoline and gunpowder.

What with the flare and movement of torches, and the flickering shadows, I could make out very little; but I did see that the English lady who had been sitting beside me in the plane was still arguing with the black gentleman, who—to my surprise—

was now wearing an Arab keffiyeh, and brandishing a submachine gun. "My great-great-great-
grandfather," he was saying, "was a King."

"Royalty," said the British lady, "must always
command respect, of a sort. However, someone sold
your great-great-great-grandfather into slavery; and
it was not *my* great-great-great-grandfather who
did it."

"It was the United States of America," said the
black.

"I rather fancy," said the lady, "it was simply
another black King."

A young Arab approached us, and observed,
"We have no quarrel with England. Our war is with
Israel.

"In two minutes everything will explode; and
then the world will learn something from us."

Another Arab came hurrying up. "What is going
on?" he demanded. "I am the leader here, not you.
The planes are not to be blown up until tomorrow
morning."

"That is by no means certifiable," said the first
Arab. "I appeal to the PLO."

"I appeal to the PFLP," cried the other.

While they were arguing, a tremendous explosion shook the air as one of the jets went up in a billow of yellow flame and black smoke. I was flung to earth, where I lay for a moment, dazed and shaken.

I was roused by a hand on my shoulder, and a familiar voice, speaking softly and urgently into my ear. "Can you stand up? There is no time to waste."

I was helped to my feet, a burnous was thrown over me, a keffiyeh wrapped around my head, and the warm, firm, familiar hand grasped mine.

"Come along then; run for it," she said.

Like two Arabs, we slipped through the confusion, the torchlight, the shadows, the darkness beyond the glare of the burning plane. Everything seemed simple and natural, as it does in a dream; I had no feeling of fear; indeed, I had no feeling at all. It didn't even occur to me to wonder how she had got there. Later, when it did occur to me to ask, it no longer mattered; and besides, by then I knew the answer anyway.

Outside the last line of torches, beyond the glare of headlights and burning fuel, a small car stood waiting for us. It looked tiny and alone in the darkness, on the dim, empty floor of the desert, with

the cold glitter of the stars overhead, and only silence around it. "Get in," she said; and following
me, threw her arms around me.

"The trouble is," she cried, "I love you. Damn."

But the next moment, she pushed me away and
settled herself firmly behind the wheel. "Enough of
that," she said. "We must be in the mountains before
sun-up."

As usual, she knew what I was going to ask, and
stopped me with a finger on my lips. "As it happens," she said, "I have a friend in Alamut."

She drove very fast, but I could see nothing, only
darkness, with now and then, as we climbed a rise,
a glimpse of a star low on the horizon. I leaned
back in my seat and closed my eyes; I surrendered
myself to the situation, whatever it was. Anne had
said—for the first time—that she loved me, though
why she should be so vexed at having said it, I
didn't know. In any case, she had said it; she loved
me, and nothing else seemed important. I didn't
know why she was there, or how she had managed
it, or whose car it was, or who her friend was in
Alamut. . . .

Alamut. The fortress home of the Assassins, of

the Old Man of the Mountain. I wondered if there was anything left of it. It was a ruin now, of course. . . .

When I opened my eyes, the light had turned gray, and we were climbing among jagged rocks, and along awesome precipices. Anne had shed her burnous and was dressed in the uniform of a British Red Cross field worker. "Well," she said: "there you are!" And she added happily,

"It will be lovely in the mountains."

I tried to tell her about the English lady who had been my seat mate on the flight from London. "That would have been my godmother, most likely," she remarked. "Lady Christopher. I went all through the Middle East with her once."

The road—which was little more than a track —grew steeper and stonier; great rocks hung above us as we wound upward, and abyss after abyss opened below. It seemed to me that I caught a glimpse now and then of something that might have been part of an old stone wall high above us, perhaps the aerie of El Jebel himself, long gone to ruin, lonely and inaccessible. . . . Meanwhile I kept waiting for the house of Anne's friend to appear;

probably a Syrian farmhouse or villa, or a made-over Turkish police station.

It never did. Instead, when it seemed as though we could go no higher, she turned the car into what I at first thought was an opening in the cliff face, until I realized, as we sped through long-rusted gates, that it was part of that same ruined wall I had glimpsed above me. I then found myself in a stone courtyard, facing an ancient but well-preserved keep, gray with moss and lichen, silent and forbidding.

Apparently we were expected, for a great iron door swung ponderously open, and I followed her into a large stone hall, from whose beams and rafters, black with age, hung a number of ancient banners, including those of Godfrey of Bouillon and Raymond of Toulouse. Along the walls were ranged all manner of weapons—claymores, scimitars, halberds, spears, battle-axes; a decorative fan of richly worked daggers hung between the antlered head of an enormous stag and a huge ram's head with noble curling horns. I saw also a Crusader's shield, a tattered and—apparently—blood-stained kaftan, a gold and ivory crucifix, and a colored print "The Wreck of the Reliance" by George Baxter.

A servant in a white burnous bowed us in. "The Master is in the library," he said, "having his breakfast."

Unlike the great hall with its stony chill and dusty medieval banners, the library proved to be warmly paneled, hung with bright prints, and with a comfortable coal fire burning in the grate. The owner of all this, the Old Man himself, rose from his breakfast table and came forward to greet us. A great, bearded fellow in his early fifties, with a bold nose and sky-blue eyes, he was dressed in a long, richly embroidered gown, and wore sandals of ordinary leather. So this, I thought, is the Old Man of the Mountain . . . Himself, and obviously a friend of Anne's.

"Well done!" he exclaimed, embracing her. "You're just in time for a spot of tea."

"Splendid," said Anne. "I'm famished." And pointing to me: "Darling, this is Euwen-Robbie. He's been hijacked, and must get back to his college almost at once."

"Ah," said Himself. "Oxford, I suppose."

"No, sir," I said. "Middleton. Near Amherst."

He shook his head regretfully. "Can't say I know it," he said. "I was at Magdalene myself. But I'm delighted to meet any friend of Niniane's."

I looked at the sharp blue eyes, the brown, bushy beard streaked with gray, the bold nose. Was this a descendant of Hasan ibn-al-Sabbah? "It's very kind of you," I said.

"Now this," said Anne, seating herself at the table and gazing happily at the array of silver dishes, "is a real breakfast. Umm . . . kidneys—kippers—eggs—sausages—muffins and strawberry jam. Heavenly."

"God's grace on the both of you," said the Old Man of the Mountain. "Allah's grace on me."

Seating himself beside her, and motioning me to join them, he took up a huge pewter tankard and drained it at a gulp. "Well, now, child," he said. "Tell us what's going on in the world."

"As if you didn't know," said Anne. "There's fighting, as always. Call it with whom you will, or where you like."

"And you," he said shrewdly; "in love, as always."

"More than ever," she said, "but I resent the 'always'; it dishonors me. Euwen is my one true love, as he has been every time. And I his; but since he has almost no history. . . ."

She swallowed a large mouthful of sausage, and bent over to pat my hand. "Don't mind him," she said comfortably. "He's known me forever.

"How about you?" she asked him. "What about yourself?"

He shrugged his massive shoulders. "I've been about my business," he said cheerfully, "which is cutting throats. Everyone to his own, eh? What else is there? It's that kind of a world, my dear, and we happen to be particularly good at it—being small, poor, murderous, and inaccessible. We're the sparrows of the world: we pick the crumbs from the tables of the warring nations.

"Beyond that, I do a bit of music on the side, and have been taking lessons on the recorder. It will be something to keep me amused in Paradise. I never cared for the thought of all those women."

A huge Irish wolfhound came padding in at the open door, and crossing the room in dignified silence, laid his head on Anne's lap. "Ah, now," said the Old Man, "Hasan remembers you. Will you have time to do some hunting? There's still fine fleece on the mountain, and maybe a bird or two."

"We shall have to be pushing on, I'm afraid," said Anne. "I thought that if I could get Euwen to Damascus . . ."

"Never think of it," said Himself. "Aim for Beirut; the Lebanese are decent people for the most part. The Syrians are helping Arafat."

"They're assassins," said Anne. "The whole bloody lot of them."

The Old Man looked sharply around the room. "Mind your tongue, child," he said. "We take pride in our name." But he arose, and threw a great arm around her shoulder. "You'll stay the day, anyway," he said, "and I'll send you off in the morning by camel, for you'll never cross the Syrian lines in that infernal machine of yours."

Summoning a servant, he had us shown to a room in which to rest and refresh ourselves after the long night's drive, "For you must be tired," he said, "what with the poor roads and all." And truth to tell, I was tired, and—I am ashamed to admit—fell asleep in the middle of making love to Anne, who forgave me in her own way by cradling my head on her bosom until I woke.

Dinner that night was laid in the great hall, with the entire band of Assassins present—or, at least, those not occupied elsewhere. Himself sat on a raised dais at the head of the hall, with Anne on one side and myself on the other, while his associates sat at two long tables below us. At the end of each, well below the salt, sat harpers, one old, one young, in long gray gowns, each with a small Irish harp on his lap.

"I thought of a round table," said the Old Man, "like that one at Camelot; and I'd have it, but the hall is too small. Ah well, we're all alike, anyway, however we happen to be; rascals and scalawags. One Richard is like another; one Bedivere is like . . ."

"He is not," said Anne.

"We all come from Adam," said the Old Man, "though the color be different and the smell. It's the color that nations can't abide in each other; that, and the language. God—praised be He—did a bad job on us at Babel; and another bad job making us like the ants that can't abide the smell of other ants either."

For the first part of the meal, which consisted of spiced eels, jugged hare, roast dove, an enormous bowl of mutton, rice, sheep's eyes and testicles, mounds of dates, olives, pomegranates, melons, tankards of stout, goblets of a resinous mountain wine, Turkish paste, and apple tarts, I was too be-mused by the strangeness of my situation, and by the din and babble—for ˙everyone seemed to be talking at once—to catch any meaningful conversa-tion. But presently, as the bowls emptied and the sweet blue smoke of hashish began to curl upward toward the flags and banners, the room grew quiet and I realized that Himself was making some sort of statement.

"The years go by," he was saying; "and it is a great thing to see them go. Like the waves of the sea, they follow one another; and the young men come and go, too, like the waves of the sea. And always they want to take charge, and make the world over. But the old men live forever; for they have been weathered by the world's sorrow. And when the young men have been weathered by sor-row, they are old men.

"Let the harpers play."

At this, the older harper rose, and holding his harp on his arm, plucked an accompaniment to the following song.

> *Lord Tancred and Count Bohemund*
> *And Godfrey of Lorraine,*
> *Did slay a thousand Saracen*

The Elixir

> *In gentle Jesus' name.*
> *But we that live in Alamut*
> *And wear the Syrian hat,*
> *Have slain Count Raymond, Tancred, and*
> *Conrad of Montserrat.*
> *And others of our brotherhood*
> *That did go forth as spies,*
> *Slew several thousand Englishmen*
> *Often to their surprise.*
> *For he that lives in Alamut,*
> *The whole world is his foe.*
> *And he shall come to Paradise*
> *When Allah wills it so.*

The applause which followed the old harper's performance was long and loud, and only ended when Anne arose, and stepping down from the head table, made her way below the salt to where the young harper sat tuning his harp, and beckoning him to rise, begged him to accompany her in the following song:

> *Love is the first thing;*
> *Love goes past.*
> *Sorrow is the next thing,*
> *Quiet is the last.*

Love is a good thing;
Quiet isn't bad;
But sorrow is the best thing
I ever had.

Later that night, in our room, I asked her if sorrow were indeed the best thing, to which she answered sweetly as best she could,

"Not at this moment, love."

But very soon she gave a cry, "Jesus!", and then rested; and after a moment, whispered,

"You took advantage of me."

And still later, lying on my breast, she murmured drowsily,

"Actually, quiet isn't bad."

In the dawn light, muffled in the costumes of the Djebal Druse, our breath frosty in the air, we mounted our camels and said goodbye to our host. "You, young Euwen," he said, holding out his hand to me, "remember that history is all around you, both behind and before, and no one can be sure he won't go stumbling onto yesterday around some corner of today. And you, Niniane, my dear, I shall see you again, if not here, then somewhere else, perhaps in Avalon. For whether we go backwards or forwards, it is all one, because it has happened. Whatever has been, is, and always will be. Keep to the east of Damascus, and strike for Baalbek, and then across Lebanon to Beirut. Go with love—and with God, or Allah, it is all one."

Two Assassins mounted on shaggy ponies accompanied us through the passes for the better part of the morning. The air was like clear ice water, the sky a blazing blue; now and then I saw, silhouetted against the sky, a single horseman with a hawk on his wrist, and heard the sharp whistle of a kestrel. Far below us, to the southwest, battles raged: Hussein, Arafat, Habash, the Kings of Hebron, Jarmuth, Lachish, Robert of Normandy, Phillip, Richard, Golda Meir. . . .

Our escort left us before noon, wheeling about on their ponies, and discharging their muskets into the air. We were at the edge of the Djebal Druse; before us stretched the desert plain of Syria, shimmering in the heat.

"Are you sure you know the way around Damascus?" I asked.

She leaned over and patted my hand. "I drove for Allenby," she said.

CHAPTER

7

"Why did you say 'damn'?" I asked.

She stared at me in surprise. "Did I say that?" she asked.

"When you said you loved me."

"Oh dear. How awful of me!"

Her face clouded, and her chin sagged a little; and for a moment, and for the first time, she no longer looked like a young girl. "I suppose," she said slowly, "because it's bound to interfere with my freedom." And she added ruefully,

"As a matter of fact, it already has done."

It was the moment, of course, to ask her how she had managed to get to Jordan before me—seeing that I had left her in Bath; but for some reason

I felt curiously disinclined. It was night on the desert; behind us the mountains of the Druse had faded into the darkness, the stars flashed down on us from the enormous sky, and the air was soft and faintly fragrant. We sat beside a small fire of brittle twigs and dried pats, and our camels were hobbled nearby. In the morning we would cross below Damascus, into Lebanon.

But in the meanwhile we were encamped on ancient ground, where once, long before Stonehenge, the armies of forgotten kingdoms had slaughtered one another. Erech, Ur, Lachish, Nineveh, Babylon . . . I felt her tremble a little beside me. "The old gods are all around us," she said. "The Baalim of the desert."

"At least," I said, "there are no tree people."

That seemed to cheer her up a little. I took her in my arms, burnous and all, and kissed her night-cold cheek. After a while she turned her face to me, and I found her lips as warm as ever. "Oh," she murmured: "damn."

We were interrupted—which was perhaps just as well—by two shapes which loomed up in the darkness outside the small perimeter of our fire, and which, coming somewhat hesitantly into the light, proved to be two young men, both with the usual long hair down around their shoulders. The larger and older of the two was dressed in a leather jacket, or baldric, on which I noticed the glint of metal, no doubt, I thought, the usual medals and chains worn by members of various motorcycle clubs. The other, of a more slender build, wore a flowered shirt or jerkin of the sort very much in favor among the clothes designers in London and Los Angeles. He also carried a shoulder pouch, a small stringed instrument like a lute, and a printed sign which read:

"Winchester."

To my surprise, Anne appeared to recognize them. "On your way home," she said. "And high time, too."

The larger of the two sank down beside the fire with a grunt of relief, and relapsed into a moody silence. The younger man sat down beside him, and laid his hand for a moment on his shoulder, as though to comfort him.

"Have you come from the fighting?" I asked.

"Where else, man?" the younger of the two replied. He sighed heavily, and spat at the fire. "A crazy trip," he said. "Far out."

After a moment or two, he rummaged in the

pouch at his side, and brought out what appeared to be a kipper and the leg of a chicken. These he offered first to his companion, but on their being refused, fell to himself. "You people going north?" he asked, his mouth full of fish.

"We're crossing into Lebanon," I said. "At daybreak."

He nodded resignedly. "We tried to get in with a camel train headed for Antioch," he said, "but they wouldn't stop." He shrugged his shoulders. "Me," he said, "I'd as lief go by sea, but Richard wants to go by land. He came by sea, and left his wife in Cypress; he wants to get home to his mother. I have no mother myself, but Richard's mother is something."

"I know," said Anne. "I've seen her."

"When I'm with Mother," said Richard suddenly, "everything is exciting and joyous. I am in my own kingdom, which is not the greatest, perhaps, but certainly the fairest. I travel about to Arundel, Stokesay, Rockingham; the larks sing every day, and everyone is happy.

"But Mother is not growing any younger."

He sighed wearily. "We shall go by way of Austria," he said; and relapsed into silence.

Presently, having finished his repast, the younger of the two men unslung his lute, and after plucking a few chords, treated us to the following song:

A king went forth with all his men;
Holy, high Jerusalem.
That Christe's land and Christe's folk
Delivered be from heathen yoke.
The Saracen in shining gold
Christe's land did bravely hold;
Holy, high Jerusalem.
Yet that great city did he win.
He smote the heathen hip and thigh,
And lifted Christe's banner high,
But England's sunne was in his eye.
Holy, high Jerusalem.
A king shall rule in England yet,
Nor by a traitor be beset,
And he shall see his own once more,
His land, his mother Eleanor,
But nevermore Jerusalem.

"Oh, do shut up," said Richard.

A moment later, he burst out: "We were doing all right until the Frenchman left us. But with brother John at home, trying to take over . . ."

"It's too much," said his companion.

"Relatives are impatient," said a voice from the darkness behind us. "They cannot wait."

Peering out through the circle of firelight, I could make out a number of shadowy forms, and it seemed to me that the fire glow gleamed and glistened on weapons and armor. "I'm afraid we're in for it," I said to Anne. "The Syrians have found us."

She gave a gasp, and then sat up very straight, and set her chin in the air. "I shall demand to see the British Consul in the morning," she declared.

A man dressed in a heavily embroidered cloak strode into the light of our fire. Like Richard, he wore his hair long, but his beard was square and speckled with gray. He was neither tall nor stoutly built, but of commanding presence; and he had about him an air of gravity and sadness. "Shalom," he said.

"He's not a Syrian," Anne whispered; "he's an Israeli." And she replied, "Shalom."

The man bowed to her, but addressed himself to the younger of the two companions. "I heard you singing," he declared. "In the desert, such sounds carry far. It was of particular interest to me, because

I, too, am a singer, and have appeared in Jerusalem. I am on my way there now, with my band."

"You're too late," said Richard. "Saladin and his Saracens are there."

"Oh God," exclaimed the stranger, "the heathen have come into mine inheritance." He hesitated a moment, and then regained his composure. "I will lift up mine eyes unto the hills," he declared, "from whence cometh my help."

"There are guerrillas in the hills," I said. "Arafat, or Habash, or both."

"I have fought in the hills before," said the stranger, "and I am not too old to fight again. And there were giants in those days.

"But you, sir," he continued, seating himself next to Richard, "did I hear you say that your brother was giving you some trouble? I, too, have had family difficulties. My son . . ."

He looked about him, an old man with the eyes of an eagle. "If they cannot have what they want at the very moment they want it," he said, "they are ready to burn the world down.

"I can wait," he said patiently. "My son could not; he rose against me. There is no reason why the young should rule the world."

"Alexander did," said Richard.

"Maybe so," said the stranger. "Although I never heard of him."

I leaned back on my hands and gazed up at the stars. The night stood over me; the same stars stared down at me as had stared down at Goliath, at the hosts of the Philistines, at Saul, at Abner; the same night that had covered the tents of the Crusaders, the mounted bowmen of the Ayubite. It seemed to me that chariots and archers swept across the heavens in shadowy tides of air, Ur and Egypt, Sargon and Rameses, cloud-shadows across the moon . . . I heard the shofar, the ram's horn of Israel, the trumpets of Nineveh, the drums of France, the pipes of Allenby—Romans, Greeks, Persians, Babylonians, Chaldeans . . .

"What a pudding," I said.

"Somehow," said Richard, "I fail to see the connection."

I explained that I was thinking about history.

"History," said the stranger. "A thousand years since Abraham offered his son Isaac to the Lord as a sacrifice. A thousand years—and my own son is killed hanging from a tree by his hair. He was so proud of his long hair."

"I must say," declared Richard, "if you don't mind, it does seem odd to hear you carry on about your son. My own father wouldn't have given a tinker's curse . . ."

"I can remember my youth," said the stranger, "in the wilderness. I remember a happy time, filled with the sense of injustice. But it was also full of love. We were like young lions."

"I, too," said Richard, "have a lion's heart."

"It is all gone now," said the stranger. "Only the old know that in the end everything goes: the sword-arm first, then the voice, then the genitals. The old accept it with resignation. The young cannot; they think that they are immortal, that it will always be springtime. But the old—One warms one's feet on the soft bosom of a maid where, earlier, one would have . . . hmm." He bowed slightly to Anne. "Forgive me, ma'am," he said; "Queen of whatever land it is you rule."

"Quite all right," said Anne.

"She is no Queen," I explained, "but a long-legged English girl . . ."

"Is she, by God?" exclaimed Richard. "The devil you say!"

"However," the old man continued, "it is when

one loses one's voice, and can no longer sing . . ."

He sighed heavily, and rose somewhat shakily to his feet. "I leave you in God's hands," he said. "Joab is waiting. I have one last journey to make." He hesitated, and shook his head sadly. "You say the Saracens are in Jerusalem?" he said. "I shall probably not sing there any more. But perhaps, some day, my son Solomon—"

8

No planes were leaving Beirut, due to the hijack-
ings, and we decided to return to England by sea;
and since the only ship sailing at that time was a
small Lebanese freighter, we booked passage on her.
However, she proved to be hot, dirty, and uncom-
fortable, and besides stopped at too many ports;
and at Palermo we left her, and managed to find
room on a sailing ship bound for Cornwall. This
vessel, built like an Arab dhow, and rigged with the
usual lateen sails, was at least airy, and not un-
comfortable.

It proved to be a happy journey. The days went
by, and the nights went by, and time came to mean
less and less to me. My term at Middleton College

rarely intruded in my thoughts; I had missed the
opening by a long shot, and I felt rather devil-may-
care about it. During the warm hours of the day we
talked, sometimes in the breeze of the foredeck,
Anne sitting up very straight and holding a parasol
over her head to shield her from the sun whose rays,
she assured me, were bad for the complexion. "In
India," she told me, "my godmother would never let
me go out without a parasol. It not only saved a
girl's skin, but discouraged intimacy. In Africa, an
Englishwoman under her parasol had the same advantage as a tribal chieftain under his umbrella.

"Unless, of course," she added, "he was a canni-
bal."

At other times we lolled beneath the awning aft,
drinking cold spiced teas, and eating small cucumber
sandwiches. At night we made love in the cabin,
while the sailors, above deck, sang Sicilian sea
chanteys.

"Are you a Catholic?" asked Anne one night.
"Or Church of England?"

I replied that I was a Jew, but that I did not
make a profession of it. "I thought there was something different about you," she murmured.

Eight days out of Palermo, we passed Trafalgar,

where a naval battle had been going on, but it was already night, and the battle was over, although we could make out distantly on the horizon the glow of burning ships. "Well," I said, "Nelson is dead, and the battle won for England."

"He was a great hero," Anne declared, "and I loved him." She remained sunk in reverie for a moment, then added, somewhat coldly, I thought,

"I could never understand his asking Hardy to kiss him."

"In the heat of battle," I remarked, "one's feelings . . . on the other hand, he might just possibly have said 'Kismet, Hardy'—remembering the glorious days following the battle of the Nile. I keep thinking of Emma; aside from her grief, what a disappointment: she could have been the mistress of a Duke."

"I could never abide her," said Anne. "Though I will admit that Fanny was a poor thing, but goodhearted—which Emma certainly was not."

I found the historian in me saying, against my better judgment: "If Nelson had lost at Trafalgar, what difference would it have made in the end?"

She regarded me with astonishment. "Why, all the difference in the world!" she exclaimed. "Victoria would never have been Queen: and we'd have had some horrid little King like Jerome. And what would have happened to the Empire?"

"You have no Empire," I reminded her. "It is all gone, anyway."

She made a gesture of impatience. "But it was there," she said. "It was part of the whole. The whole dreadful, shining, bloody, glorious story. Yours too, my dear."

And she added firmly,

"I could never have loved a Frenchman."

After a while she said more gently,

"I suppose that you love me."

"Yes," I said. I wanted to say something convincing about beauty and youth, but I couldn't find the words. "The way I feel," I said, "is something completely new to me."

"Love is always new," she declared. "It is like the Spring; as though each time there had never been such blossoming, such an April . . . so much sadness, so much joy . . ."

She laid her hand on mine. "I love you, too," she said.

But the implication was plain enough: she had loved before, and I preferred not to think about it.

A few days later, in the sun on the foredeck, and

with the parasol over her head, she returned to the subject of religion. Behind us, the lateen sail strained in the steady wind from the south, and the dim blue bulk of Portugal lay low on the horizon to our right. "Do you believe in God?" she asked. "Some people claim that He is dead."

I looked around me at the sea and the sky, at the bright sparklet of sunlight on the waves, at the exquisite girl beside me, and I replied:

"God cannot be dead. Since He is the fountain of life, He must be present wherever life is present. You can't get something out of nothing, not even with a trick hat."

"I used to see it done," said Anne. "At Christmas parties. It was usually a rabbit, or a colored handkerchief."

"Yes," I said. "I did, too."

I continued: "Do you know why God exists? It is because behind every question there is only another question. One asks, What is time? And one answers that it rests in eternity like water in a basin. And then one asks: In what does the basin rest?

"Or one says that there was a great explosion of gas, which created the galaxies; but then one is obliged to ask: Where did the gas come from?

"In the end, there has to be Something, beyond the last question."

"All that," said Anne, "is merely confusing. I prefer to think of religion as doing one's best here on earth. As my nanny used to say:

> *Do the work that's nearest,*
> *Though it's dull at whiles;*
> *Helping, when you meet them,*
> *Lame dogs over stiles.*

"My darling," I said, "I am convinced that you have made up this nanny of yours out of whole cloth."

"I have done nothing of the kind!" she exclaimed indignantly. "I have never made up anything in my life."

She gave a sudden, anxious, childish sigh. "Sometimes," she said, "I do make things up. But not my nanny."

Schools of porpoises accompanied us, their long, arching leaps cleaving the water ahead of us, scattering slim sprays of foam around us. Off Aveiro we passed through the sardine fishing boats with great eyes painted on their prows, and hove to, to exchange leatherwork, cream of tartar, and bolts of silk for jars of olive oil, tobacco, and oranges.

Anne had found a mandolin in the cabin, and with the young moon laying thin silver lozenges on the black water, she sang me old sea chanteys such as "A-Roving," and bits from *The Pirates of Penzance* and *Pinafore,* the "Eton Boating Song" and "Blow the Wind Southerly"—

Blow the wind southerly, southerly, southerly,
Blow the wind south o'er the bonny blue sea.
Blow the wind southerly, southerly, southerly,
Blow, bonny breeze, my lover to me.

Next day the sun shone blindingly bright, and the wind fell away. Toward noon the porpoises left us, and I became aware of an air of concern among the crew. Anxious looks were turned toward the west, where a grayish haze began to form; the sails were reefed, the awning furled and put away, lines and gear made secure, and hatches battened down. The air grew more and more oppressive; there was no doubt that a storm was headed our way, one of those sudden summer gales such as had struck the galleons of the Armada in 1588.

The Elixir

I have always been frightened of storms; as a child I used to quake at the thunder (the lightning only startled me) and pull the sheets up over my head. It was the violence. . . . But, except for a tornado which is sudden and over very soon, or a hurricane which is really a sea storm, there is never quite the same fear on land as at sea, sandwiched as one is between the two outrageous elements, water and air.

Anne, on the contrary, seemed to come more vividly alive in the face of danger; it was not so much that she welcomed it, as that she appeared to accept it as part of her destiny, and—in a rather touching and gallant sort of way—defy it. Seated cross-legged on her bunk, with shining eyes, she seemed an eager child, alert and obstinate.

"Euwen-Robbie," she said, "this will be a great storm. And if anything happens—"

"Pray God nothing will," I said. "The ship is solid, and the crew used to bad weather."

But she only smiled at me. "Pray God, Robbie?" she asked gently. "In what language?"

And taking up her mandolin, she began to sing:

> *The last Queen of England*
> *Sits on her throne,*

And doom moves
In the cold stone.
She holds her scepter,
She wears her crown,
But evil gathers
In village and town.
The last brave admiral
Goes below.
The night has taken
Horatio.
And where the nations
Speak together
Is cold regard
And bitter weather.
The bells ring
In the empty steeple.
They bring no hope
To frightened people.
With our last breath
Let us try to pray
For those we love,
To whom we may.

The first squall hit us with a sudden downpour, followed by a violent blow of wind. The dhow reeled, and I felt the solid lurch of fear in my stomach before the ship righted herself and, still quivering, with her sea anchor out, rose to the cresting waves. I could feel the pressure of the storm in my ears; the wind seemed to have sucked the air out of the cabin, it was hard to breathe. In the next half hour it seemed to increase in violence; finally there was a dreadful lurch as the yard broke, trailing wood and wild-flying canvas over the deck, which caused the dhow to broach to and present her side to the sea, which all but overturned her. We were flung to the cabin floor, and a moment later I heard a second snapping sound and muffled cries from the deck, and realized from the sudden crazy gyrations of the ship that the great steering oar must have given way. Green, foaming water poured into the cabin, and Anne stared at me with frightened eyes.

"They really mean it this time," she said. "They really do."

I put my mouth down close to her ear. "I'm going on deck," I shouted over the sound of wind and water. "If the steering oar has gone, they'll need everyone they can get."

She nodded, and rose to her feet, apparently meaning to go with me. "I wish you wouldn't," I said; but she didn't hear me. "At least," I said, "put this on."

And wrapping an old life jacket around her, I kissed her and held her for a moment. "I love you," I said. "After all, there's been that."

She nodded again; her cheek was cold as ice. "Take care of yourself," she said. "Hold on to something."

I went up the ladder to the deck. I don't know what I had expected to see; actually, I could see nothing, only a wild tumble of white and green water, and the wind lashing it past me. There was a steady howling in the air, and I could just see Anne coming up out of the cabin behind me, her hair whipping crazily about her face. I started to make my way toward the stern, where there seemed to be a gathering of vague forms, but the wind lifted me, gave me a buffet that knocked me to one side, and at that moment a mountainous wave rose above me; I had just time to see it towering over me like a nightmare mountain, and then I was overboard, floundering in the sea, alone, out of sight, out of earshot, out of all hope. . . .

The last thing I can remember was trying to shout "Anne . . . Anne . . . !"

CHAPTER

9

I seemed to swim upward, very slowly and uncomfortably, to consciousness—and found myself in a very soft bed, with a vaguely remembered face bending over me. "There," said a voice; "that's better."

Almost at once, I fell asleep again. It would be another twenty-four hours before I would know where I was, and what had happened to me.

I had been washed up on the Cornish coast more dead than alive; and being found among the rocks by some fishermen, had been carried to the home of the apothecary at Camelford, and there revived, in a feather bed, with hot stone bottles around me, and infusions of mulled wine. The apothecary, as it turned out, was that same Mr. Jones whom I had met once before in the bookshop, and who had sold me the copy of Zimmer's *Nennius Vindicatus*. "I thought you were a bookseller," I declared.

His gnomelike face broke into a smile. "Let me make you a nice cup of tea," he said; and leaving the room, presently returned with a steaming mug from which arose a comforting fragrance. I recognized the odor of camomile, and a slight taste of ginger; whatever else he had put in it, I do not know, but I very soon began to feel better.

Seating himself by my bedside, he studied me over his fingertips. "If I remember rightly," he remarked, "there is, among the *Curiosities* of the monk Derwent of Cadmium, the story of a sailor washed overboard in a storm at sea and delivered in good condition to the Lady of Penzance (who may have been Ygraine, daughter of King Mark) by a large fish or sea monster, possibly—although he does not insist on it—a porpoise or dolphin. In your case, however, I have to tell you that you came ashore attached to a floating mine, which failed to explode on contact."

"How does it happen," I asked, "that I find you an apothecary, and not a bookseller?"

Mr. Jones laughed shyly. "I am both, actually," he said. "In a small community such as this, it is best to have more than one pot on the stove. I am also something of a doctor, although not licensed; and, of course, something of an historian. And I do bits of magic at private parties."

I thought of Anne, and a lump formed itself in my throat. "Can you take a rabbit out of a hat?" I asked.

"The hat trick is not very difficult," he replied, "provided one has the right hat for it. And to draw cards and other magic things out of the air . . . there's little to that, actually. Though to turn oneself into a stuffed owl is a horse of another color."

He stopped, and frowned. "I find," he said, "that as I grow older, I have a tendency to mix metaphors. You must forgive me."

"I shan't ask you how old you are," I declared.

"Thank you," he said. "I had rather you didn't. One likes to maintain a certain privacy. Americans, I find, have very little reserve; always asking questions. Personal questions. Like what did one do in the war, or does one know the address of a good doctor? What beastly business is it of theirs?"

"They are inquisitive about history," I reminded him, "having so little of their own."

"Ah yes," he said. "Maybe so. You have a point."

"At any rate," I remarked, "I've been having quite a lot of history myself lately."

"I dare say," he replied. And added reprovingly, "But it has all been English history, you see."

"Not King David!" I exclaimed.

He looked puzzled for a moment. "I'm afraid I don't quite follow you," he said. "Do you mean the son of Jesse—or of George the Fifth? *His* name, by the way, was Edward."

"I mean David, the son of Jesse," I replied, "King of the Jews, and father of Solomon."

"Ah," said Mr. Jones thoughtfully: "the Jews. They were related to the Celts, you know—though removed by several thousands of years and various migrations. However, the likenesses are unmistakable. In addition, members of the tribes of Dan and Asher, being seafarers, visited Britain in the ninth century B.C., either as salesmen, or as vacationers; and many settled here, some because of business opportunities, and others rather than face the long sea voyage home. And some say that the Scythians were Jews."

"Well, then," I said, drowsily, "if I haven't had a long history as an American, at least I've had a long history as a Jew."

And I fell asleep again.

I cannot say that I dreamed; rather, it seemed to me that I was actually in Atlantic City, New Jersey, during the course of a beauty contest in which Anne was entered not as Miss England, but as The Lady of the Lake. Dressed in her bathing suit, she presented the most delicious sight imaginable; firm-bosomed, small-waisted, with creamy shoulders, long straight legs, and firmly rounded hips, she seemed perfection itself. I woke up weeping.

For the thought that she might not have survived the storm struck me with sudden force; what if there were no Anne in the world any more? I realized that I had to find her, if she was living; and—if she were not—my life was as good as over. She had said that each new love was like another Spring; but Spring melts into Summer, and Summer fades into Fall, and I could have told her that only one love in a man's life can last him through the seasons.

"How can I find her?" I asked Mr. Jones. "How can I find out if she is still alive? Even her name— Niniane Mellers . . . I'm not at all sure . . ."

The apple-faced man smiled gently. "Mellers," he said admiringly: "Well, why not? It is as good a name as any. Though I've known her by different."

He went away, and returned in a little while with a newspaper. "You will be happy to hear that she is alive and well," he announced. "According to the *Tatler*, she is enjoying a visit with the Queen at Ashby de la Zouch."

"Then," I said, "that's where I'm going as soon as I can. If you'll just tell me how to get there—or arrange some sort of transportation—"

"As a matter of fact," said Mr. Jones, "I rather think I should enjoy the trip myself. That is, of course, if you don't mind. I shall accompany you; we will go together."

I had imagined that I could rent a car in Camelford, but I was mistaken; and for a while it looked as though we might have to go by horse and carriage, at least as far as Princetown; but in the end Mr. Jones managed to come up with an ancient two-cylinder de Dion Bouton touring car complete with hand crank, acetylene lamps, and a wickerwork tonneau which opened from the rear like an Irish jaunting cart. "Good heavens," I exclaimed when I saw it, "wherever did you conjure this relic from?"

"From the past," said Mr. Jones simply. "And I'm a proper wizard to have found it at all. Have no fear; it will get us there in good order just the same."

With a steak-and-kidney pie, some meat pasties, a wedge of cheese, and half a dozen bottles of stout packed away in the rear, we set forth with a great deal of popping and grinding, which seemed to astonish those who saw us, for they stood staring after us and scratching their heads, as though they'd never seen a motor car before. "At least," I said, "they've probably not seen one like this, for it must be well over sixty years old."

"Ah, well, do you see," said Mr. Jones, "they made things to last in those days."

And certainly, as he had promised, it carried us along; and I soon found that I liked the sense of freedom it gave me, with the air on my face and on my legs, and enjoyed our mild progress through the countryside, and the lofty view from my high seat next to the driver. Mr. Jones drove, for he thought himself probably more in tune with such an early contraption than I might be. He had, I discovered, a tendency to slow down to a crawl, almost to a stop, when anything approached us from the opposite direction, but fortunately there was little traffic on the road, and most of it was going our way.

That night we lay at the Crown and Garter Inn at Taunton. We were lucky to get a room, for a handbill circulated in town—a copy of which I had already seen posted along the way at Widdicombe —announced the presence at the Crown and Garter of the Strolling Players, a group connected with Mr. Burbage's Blackfriar's Theatre, and advertising a performance of *The Mouse Trap,* or *Gonzago and Baptista,* in the Assembly Rooms of the Town Hall on Tuesday next, "the very same company as was recently brought over from Danemark, where they had performed this same piece by Royal Command."

Hearing from the innkeeper that the company was rehearsing that evening in the basement of the Masonic Temple, we strolled down that way after supper, to look in at them. From the doorway, where we stood, they seemed ordinary enough, though on the whole rather young; men and women

—if they were women—all wore their hair long, and were dressed in jeans and old sweaters or burlap blouses. They were seated around a table; a candle, stuck in an empty wine bottle, threw a faint and wavering light on their faces. They were listening intently to the director, a balding, middle-aged man with a neatly trimmed beard. He was, apparently, dissatisfied with one of the actors.

"It out-Herods Herod," he said. "Give it smoothness; suit the action to the word. Hold the mirror up to nature. Nor do not saw the air too much with your hand. Speak the speech, I pray you, as I pronounced it."

" 'Trippingly on the tongue,' " I said to myself, as we closed the door and started back to the inn.

"Pardon?" said Mr. Jones.

"Nothing," I said. "Nothing at all.

"Just that the director had auburn hair, and hazel eyes."

Mr. Jones gave me an enigmatic look. "Ah, yes," he said. "Yes, he did. I was not aware that you had noticed."

Mist was thick on the roads next morning, and the towns we passed through were shrouded, empty, and still, as though withdrawn from the world. It

was eerie to be driving through an unknown countryside, unable to see for more than a few yards on
either side; but my impatience to find Anne was so
great that I preferred to grope my way north rather
than suffer any further delays. Mr. Jones, who was
doing the driving, seemed not to mind; as a matter
of fact, I had the feeling that his thoughts were
elsewhere, and that he drove without paying any
attention to the scenery or the lack of it.

But although I was unable to see much of the
landscape, I was well aware of sounds; and more
than once I mentioned the fact that I seemed to
hear hoofbeats and the lumbering rumble of a
coach, the crack of a whip, the creak of wheels, and
even a postillion's horn. "Why not?" said Mr. Jones
at last; "since we are on the Great North Road?"

There were other sounds, too; on one occasion,
the rattle of musketry, and the keen of bagpipes
came faintly down the wind; and once we stopped
at a crossroads to let a regiment of lancers go by,
half-seen, shadowy forms, spurs and bridles jin-
gling, kettledrums beating and pennons fluttering—
out of the mist and into it again, from nowhere into
nowhere. "I dare say they're on their way to join
Raglan," said Mr. Jones; and he added smugly,

The Elixir

"Now there's a bit of history for you."

I didn't answer; but I thought to myself that what actually occurs is history, and what one likes to remember is legend, and that there is a vast difference between the two. For history is the record—or what one is able to salvage in the confusion of the actual happening—of man's mistakes; and legend is the well-worn oft-told tale of his glories. And I thought, too, that the truth lies somewhere in between, and one is no more honest than the other, but one is dearer. And the further off in time, the softer it glows.

It was Marlowe who gave that faithless Argive wife a face that launched a thousand ships; and it was Tennyson who turned the mindless slaughter of England's finest horsemen into a poem. And Anne— who had created her own little village of Saffron Orcas, out of . . . what? A child's dream . . . a fairy tale.

In the night of the soul, that little glow, fox-fire though it be, provides an only comfort.

Whether my own musing was at fault (although, having no map or knowledge of the roads, I couldn't have been of use in any case) or Mr. Jones's reveries, whatever they were, we somehow managed to take the wrong fork beyond Salisbury, and found ourselves in the late afternoon approaching Sevenoaks instead of Kenilworth as we had planned. And found our way impeded, besides—if not actually blocked—by a considerable number of men, some singly and others in groups of a dozen or more, all going in the same direction as ourselves, toward a meeting place somewhere nearby.

They were for the most part, and at first glance, the same long-haired and bearded fellows whose appearance was familiar to me on the campus at Middleton and on television; but a closer look showed many of them to be older, and I noticed that there were no women among them. They were dressed in the usual rags, rough smocks and blouses; and some carried signs, while others carried scythes and billhooks. The signs, which were obviously home-made, contained such mottoes as: *Free John Ball, Housing for All,* and *The Poll Tax Is Unfair.*

Leaving the car by the side of the road, we made our way toward the fire, where a large group had gathered around their leader, a burly, bearded fellow whose face, flushed by the firelight, reflected both determination and the excitement of the moment. No one appeared to notice us, for which, I confess, I was grateful, as the mood of the gathering was anything but friendly.

By overhearing bits of conversation here and there, I discovered that the meeting had been called to protest the arrest of John Ball, a popular Leftist preacher, who was being held in gaol at Maidstone.

I pressed as close to the leader as I could, hoping to catch his speech, which was continually being interrupted by the arrival of newcomers who came onto the meadow with cries of "Fair Ball!" and "Freedom Now!" At times groups of his followers would break into a chant: "John the Miller grinds small, small, small"; to which other groups would reply,

"The King's son of Heaven shall pay for all."

I could hear enough of the leader's remarks to realize that he was advocating peace of body and joy of heart, fellowship in heaven and on earth, equal opportunity for all, repeal of the groat tax, abolition of Parliament, and an end to the Establishment. "When Adam delved," he demanded, "and Eve span, who was then the gentleman?"

"Aye, who?" cried his followers. And,

"John Ball hath rungen thy bell."

Standing on an empty keg, his clenched fist raised in defiance, the speaker continued:

"They strip the clothes from our daughters, to pay for their pleasures! There is no justice in this country for those whose honest toil hath enriched the land. They keep us in rags while they deck themselves in fine silks and satins; they dine on sweetmeats while we dine on slops."

"Wat Tyler!" cried the crowd. "Right on!"

"We have been serfs and villeins too long!" he shouted. "Those days are over. Meaning no disrespect to the Crown, I say that them as stands in our way will find their heads stuck on pikes on London Bridge. The revolution has begun. In Cambridge, they have burned the charters of the university. In Essex, in Fobbing and Brentwood, Jack Straw and his men have already killed one judge and members of the jury. If we cannot have justice by courtesy, we shall have it by force!"

To this the crowd responded with roars of approval. "On to Maidstone!" they cried.

"Power to the people!"

"Down with Uncle Tom Cobleigh and all!"

Brandishing his clenched fist, their leader exclaimed,

"We shall overcome!"

He then added, in a lower voice, as an aside, "There will be no laws in England saving those I declare."

One by one his followers came to the fire, seized a lighted brand, and with torches flaring, started down the road toward Maidstone. As their voices diminished in the distance, we could still hear them chanting:

"John the Miller grinds small, small, small;

The King's son of Heaven shall pay for all."

We found ourselves alone, beside the dying fire. Slowly and soberly, we left the field, climbed into our ancient motor car, and headed down the road in the opposite direction from which we came.

We drove in silence for several hours. At last Mr. Jones gave a sigh. " 'Aye, not with glory,' " he declaimed, " 'but with peace, May the long summers find me crowned.' "

"That's Euripides, of course," he said. "From the *Medea*. In the Gilbert Murray translation. Oxford University Press, 1906."

"I know," I said. He continued:

For gentleness—her very sound
Is magic, and her usages
All wholesome; but the fiercely great
Hath little music on his road,
And falleth, when the hand of God
Shall move, most deep and desolate.

"A good man, Murray," he said. "Rather under-estimated, in my opinion; not as a scholar, mind you, but as a poet. The rot you find nowadays in the reviews—published, too, in hard-cover; I can't make head nor tail of it half the time, myself. And the language! Appalling!"

"An Anglo-Saxon revival, supposedly," I explained.

"Ah," said Mr. Jones. "But the language, in the early days, had so few words in it; why revive a period of poverty?"

It must have been nearly midnight when we heard a sudden "thunk," followed by a loud hissing sound, and the car lurched and came to a stop, slanting a little to one side. I knew, of course, what had happened; one of our tires had given out. Mr. Jones climbed down to assess the damage, and discovered to his chagrin that an arrow had pierced

The Elixir

the right forward tire, causing a puncture, and that further progress was impossible. Holding the arrow up to the light of the headlamps, he gave a low whistle. "A gray goose feather," he muttered; and peering about him in the darkness, he called out indignantly,

"All right, then, John; come out, wherever you are.

"I should have known," he said to me, sniffing the air, "where we were by the smell."

And indeed the night air did have an odor of dank vegetation, fungus, rotted trees, and moldy earth, as well as the living bark of trees, all of which came together in a rich forest fragrance. "Sherwood Forest," I said. "Of course."

A moment later, a tall, lean, hulking figure came silently out of the darkness, and into the light of our headlamps. "I didn't know it was you, Myrdin," he said. "I'd like my arrow back, if you please. Times are hard, and good shafts aren't easy to come by."

Mr. Jones handed the arrow back to him. "Where is Huntingdon?" he asked. "And Tuck?"

"Well, now," said John, "they're at Ashby, to keep an eye on Marian."

Mr. Jones appeared surprised. "What on earth is the Maid doing at Ashby?" he asked.

"Well, then, she's entered at the Court of Beauty," said John. "But what are you doing here yourself, Myrdin? So far from Cornwall?"

Mr. Jones explained that we had come to Ashby to view the proceedings at the Court of Beauty, and introduced me to John, whose other name was Little. "Mr. Irwin is a friend of Niniane of Avalon," he explained, "and he is anxious to meet with her again."

At this John's face took on a sober expression. "Then he has come in good time," he said, "or maybe not, for I have heard a few things; and they say the contest is already decided in favor of Somerset, and King John is to have his pick of the others, and after him the Sheriff; and it's for that Locksley has gone to keep an eye on Marian."

"Ah well," said Mr. Jones, "in any case, we can go no farther tonight, or until we get this tire repaired."

"I'm truly sorry for what I done," said Little John contritely, "but since there's no help for it, I suggest you spend the night with us in the Greenwood, and in the morning we get a wheelwright to fix the wheel for you, and you be on your way."

Since it not only seemed like a sensible arrangement, but was, besides, the only one offered us, we accepted the outlaw's invitation, and following Little John through the forest for some ten or fifteen minutes, found ourselves in a small glade, made warm and cheerful by a good fire, around which the rest of the band were gathered in various attitudes of relaxation. Being made welcome, we seated ourselves among them, and after a satisfying meal of roast venison washed down with flagons of ale, we stretched ourselves out on the greensward, and despite Little John's disturbing though ambiguous remark about the contest, I must say that we slept very well.

10

The next morning, a wheelwright from Swadling-cote having been engaged, we were able to repair the tire, and were presently on our way to Ashby de la Zouch where the Queen's Court of Love was holding its Contest of Beauty. The trouble with the tire having held us up, we were somewhat late in arriving, and the contest was under way, the knights and their squires already in the field, and the spectators in their seats behind and on either side of the royal box.

It was, I confess, a marvelous scene, of bright colors under a windy sky; gold and scarlet, the gleam of burnished armor, pennons and banners streaming, plumes tossing, horses rearing and plunging, and the spectators arrayed in all the colors of the rainbow; and in the midst of them, under a canopy of gold cloth, with the lion banner of England on one side and the lily banner of France on the other, the Queen herself, Eleanor of Aquitaine, and her Ladies.

There was no mistaking the beauty, the vivacity, of this famous woman; watching her, I was reminded that it was in her court that the art of lyric poetry had flourished and romantic love been born, with its emphasis on chivalry and *gentillesse;* that there, too, the Gay Art of the troubadours (her son Richard was one) was nurtured, the Adoration of the Virgin encouraged, and the worship of woman accepted as man's first duty, after his duty to the Pope. There knights competed in jousts, each sporting some favor, a kerchief or a glove belonging to his lady to whose purity he was devoted, the winning knight having as sole reward the honor of crowning his lady Queen of Beauty.

As we watched, from the edge of the meadow, which was as close as we could get to the Field of Honor, there was a flourish of trumpets, after which a troubadour (whom I recognized from my night on the Syrian desert) stepped forward, and after bowing to the Queen and to the nobles present, first tuned his harp with a golden key which he wore around his neck, and then launched into the following *ottima* and *sestina* in praise of beauty:

Of seven virtues has my true love seven:
She is more cunning than the hummingbird,
More warm and rosy than the light of heaven,
More bright and changing than a poet's word.
The rose is not more velvet, not the rose,
The thrush at evening does not sing as sweet,
All gaiety and joy are where she goes,
And follow dancing at her dancing feet.
Yet of these virtues still another charm
Has bound my life to hers in gentle bands:
When from her eyes with love or with alarm
The very soul looks out between her hands,
Then do I see but for a moment's worth,
All that is good and kind upon this earth.

For to the lover beauty is his love,
His heart's dear mistress ever at his side;
She is the blue bright wind of heaven above,
The light of evening on the valleys wide.
She is the sea, she is the swifter tide
Of narrower waters, and the forest green;

The Elixir

In all his courses, beauty is his guide,
She goes before him, she is heard and seen,
And has a body. Let the lover tell
Whose voice he hears in music's sweetest part;
He knows the face of beauty, knows it well.
She is his friend, the treasure of his heart,
That on the earth like benediction pours
A light he loves, a spirit he adores.

After acknowledging the applause, the singer bowed low before the Queen, who placed in his hands a small purse containing his royalties. There was another flourish of trumpets, and the knights then formed two lines, between which the contestants for the Crown of Beauty advanced one by one, to the accompaniment of a roll of drums, first curtsying before the royal box, and then turning to the right and to the left before taking their places on the low dais in front of and below her Majesty. Each one, as she advanced, was introduced by the Royal Herald, Clarenceaux King of Arms, who stood with the Pursuivants Rouge-Croix and Rouge-Dragon to the right of the Grand Marshal, in this case the Queen's cousin by marriage, the Earl of Northumberland.

"The Lady Cecily De Vere."

"The Lady Angela Howard."

"Blanche des Bois Epais."

At each introduction the spectators applauded, occasionally breaking into whistles of appreciation and encouragement.

"The Countess of Surrey."

"Elaine de Lacy."

I felt Mr. Jones at my side make a movement of impatience. "Women were better looking in my day," he remarked. "I remember the young Eleanor when she was Queen of France; a delightful girl. She would have made these feminine trifles look like overgrown children, which is what, in fact, they are. A woman's beauty lies less in the arrangement of her features than in the gentleness and vivacity of her air, the mixture of mirth and shyness, the wonder that looks out of her eyes, the modesty and pride to be seen in the curve of her neck and the thrust of her bosom. In short, in that mystery which touches the heart as well as the loins, and causes young men to write rondels and madrigals.

"These present-day beauties are all alike, one custard pudding after another, each topped by the same meringue."

"All except Anne," I said.

"Ah well," said Mr. Jones comfortably; "our girl has been around a long time."

I was about to reply to this—as it seemed to me—denigrating remark, when the voice of the Royal Herald, Clarenceaux King of Arms, announced,

"Mistress Niniane of Saffron Orcas."

Her head up, her chin in the air, gazing at the sky, Anne passed through the line of knights and made her obeisance to the Queen. My heart gave a great leap in my breast, and my throat turned dry; I thought that I had never seen anything so lovely, and I would have started forward across the field if Mr. Jones hadn't restrained me.

To see one's love across a crowded room is a secret and strange delight; but here I saw her, gowned as never before, in such a multitude of knights-at-arms, in such a company of beauty, amid such trappings of heraldry and regal magnificence, that I felt humbled, and a little sad and bashful, and (as Anne would have said) slightly colonial.

After the last of the contestants, including Maid Marian, had been seated, the jousts began, and several knights were left sprawled upon the field;

unhorsed that day were Sir Bors, Sir Lionel, the Lord of the Castle Doloureuse, the Norman Baron Fortmain, Hughes de Lacy, the Earl of Chester, and Philip of Kenilworth, who wore the colors of Miss De Vere.

I kept my eyes glued to Anne's face, which expressed now hope and now anxiety; when her champion Sir Bedivere was borne to earth, she first covered her eyes, then lifted them in despair to the sky, while her lips framed the words,

"Oh heaven! No, really! Actually!"

At last when only two champions were left, a knight in black armor whose shield bore no design, and the Queen's own champion, Edmond of Perigord, the Grand Marshal, the Earl of Northumberland, threw down his baton, signifying an end to the tournament. "Why is that?" I asked, "since the issue has not been finally decided?" Mr. Jones replied that it was not considered good policy to allow the Queen's champion to be overthrown. "In any case," he said, "it was all arranged beforehand."

Edmond of Perigord and the Black Knight now approached the royal box, dipping their spears to the Queen, who placed on the Black Knight's spear the crown of beauty, while offering her own champion a golden rose. The Black Knight, still with his visor closed, then offered the crown to a thus-far unregarded young lady, the daughter of a landed gentleman of Lancashire. The young lady so chosen at once turned pale and burst into tears; moments later, attempting to express her thanks, her faltering words were drowned out in a tumult of indignation from the stands, and boos and cries from the field itself; in the commotion, several contestants fainted, while others brandished their fists in the direction of the royal box, from which Eleanor had already withdrawn.

Meanwhile, throughout the hubbub, I had kept my eyes on Anne, when all at once I was distracted by a sudden disturbance in the stands where several of Nottingham's deputies were attempting to take hold of Maid Marian, who was being defended by Little John and a splendid fellow in green whom I took to be Locksley himself, Earl of Huntingdon. The deputies had, indeed, managed to surround the three, and all escape seemed cut off, when the Earl put a golden whistle to his lips and blew a shrill blast which was answered from the far end of the field, and a moment later one of the soldiers fell forward with an arrow in his breast. His companions drew back in momentary dismay, which allowed the Earl, the Maid, and Little John to make a tremendous leap over an entire row of benches, and the next moment they were lost to sight in the crowd.

They had no sooner disappeared, than I was electrified to hear Anne's voice raised in a cry of terror: "Euwen; to me!"—and turning hastily toward where I had last seen her, was shocked to find her seat empty, and no sight of her anywhere. "Good God!" I cried; "they've taken Anne!"

At this, Mr. Jones became more agitated than usual, and shaking his head, exclaimed,

"This is indeed something for which I was not prepared."

But after a moment's thought, he added more cheerfully, "Ah well, not to worry. I have taught her a few tricks over the years; one of them is to keep her hands behind her back. It is very offputting, as a matter of fact: whoever has her, he will almost surely be kept in a fume until morning. The main thing is to find out where she is being held."

He wet his finger in his mouth, and held it up in the air. "The wind is from the east," he declared, "which should bring fog by morning, but a clear night. That should suit us very well. Meanwhile, the best thing we can do is to return to Locksley and his band in the Greenwood, for I am sure that they can tell us where the kidnappers have taken our friend, who they are, and what they want of her. Though—" and he gave a slight shudder—"of the latter, there can be no reasonable doubt; despite her years, she is an attractive woman. Possibly we might be able to enlist the aid of Locksley himself, and some of his men; they are very talented with the longbow, as you have seen; and they have little reason to like the Sheriff of Nottingham—if it turns out that he is Niniane's abductor, and not, God forbid, King John himself, which would be another kettle of fish altogether."

As Mr. Jones had expected, Locksley and his band had already returned to the Greenwood, carrying Maid Marian with them; and there, seated before the fire, we also found the Black Knight enjoying a bowl of stew. He had finally doffed his helm; and I was not too much surprised to discover the features of that same Richard with whom Anne and I had spent such an interesting night in the Syrian desert. However, he seemed older, and his hair was not as long.

"Well, well, my friend," he said when he saw me, "we seem to have a way of meeting in unexpected places. But where is the damsel? Or have you and she parted company?"

When I told him that Anne had been abducted, he shook his head. "That won't do," he said severely. "It won't do at all. It's not the thing. Do you think the Sheriff has her in custody? In that case, I must say he has greatly exceeded his authority."

When I expressed the fear that Anne might be in the hands of his brother instead, his face grew dark, and he hit the palm of his hand with his balled fist. "No!" he exclaimed. "That is really too bad. John gets everything."

"Pardon me, Sire," said Friar Tuck, "but whatever made you give the crown to such a common young lady, when everyone expected it to go to the Howard girl, or at least to Cecily De Vere?"

Richard sighed. "I need the commons," he said, "and I need Lancashire. I am not as foolish politically as you think."

He turned apologetically to me. "I should really have given the crown to your own lady," he said, "and left Miss Smith for John. He's had all the rest of them, anyway." He sighed again, heavily.

"Damme," he said. "I suppose we shall have to get your damsel out of hock, wherever she is. Where do you think she is, Hunt?"

"Both John and the Sheriff lie tonight at Belvoir Castle," said the Earl, "and she must be with one or t'other. We've been in and out of there before . . . there's a way of shinnying up a drainpipe . . . and we should have no trouble, once we know which apartment she is in. As for the men-at-arms, guards, and so forth—all you have to do is show yourself, and my fellows will account for the rest."

"Very well," said Richard glumly. "We'll ride at dawn. I suppose I shall have to tell my brother off. . . . Frankly, I was in no hurry to do so, for I enjoy these evenings in the forest, with the merry men, and the singing and all. I detest court life. However, my mother seems to have grown over-fond of John these past years, and that won't do either. I'm certain that the two of them had promised Angela Howard the crown—and she can't sing a note."

"Her father," remarked Friar Tuck sagely, "can field a thousand horse."

Richard gave the Friar a look at once wise and sad. "I had a thousand horse before Jerusalem," he said. "But so had Saladin. In the end, one remembers other things: the sound of chanting in the great cathedrals, the songs of the nightingales in Cypress . . . a Saracen girl singing in the Bazaar at Haifa."

He remained for a while sunk in reverie before the fire. But presently his mood changed, and he looked up with animation. "I thought Blondel did rather well," he said; "didn't you? That *ottima* and *sestina* of his; what? Brought it over from Italy, I shouldn't wonder."

"By the bye," he said, turning to me, "whoever was this fellow Bedivere? He wore your lady's colors, I believe. Took a tumble, too."

"Oh," I said casually, "he was just somebody out of Malory."

"Ah well," said Richard: "Malory. I've never been there, myself."

He emptied his bowl of stew and stood up. "I think I shall go back to France," he said. "There is a lot of music in France."

11

We reached Belvoir Castle in the early dawn, and it being overset with fog, as Mr. Jones had prophesied, we had no difficulty in approaching the walls which rose dark and grim into the concealing mist. Since Robin Hood's men had long ago found a place where it was possible to ford the moat, we waded silently across, and huddled in the shadow of the keep itself, hearing above us the tread of armed sentries on the battlements. One of Locksley's men climbed the drainpipe as planned, slipped into the castle, and was presently able to open a small postern gate for us, giving onto the kitchens, which we crossed in single file and absolute silence except for a low cough from one of the men who was

momentarily overcome by the odor of boiled cab-
bage and suet from the night before.

Coming to a low door, we found ourselves on a
flight of stone steps, and felt our way upward in the
dark. It was bitterly cold; I had no idea where I
was or where I should presently find myself, and
would certainly have been overcome by fright except for the reassuring knowledge that Robin and
his men were somewhere ahead of me, and Mr.
Jones behind.

But when we came out at last onto a stone
landing or vestibule, from which a series of gal-
leries appeared to lead outward in every direction,
there was no sign of Locksley and his band; we
were alone. The night torches in their wall rings
were all but burned out, and the early dawn light
showed gray in the high, narrow windows. All was
silent; the castle was still asleep, which was our
good fortune; but where was Anne? And with
whom?

With my heart making more noise in my chest
than my feet on the stone floor, we went down the
largest gallery, listening at each door, but heard
only snores, and returned disappointed in anxious
haste to try another which offered us nothing but

empty storerooms. The dawn light grew brighter, and my apprehensions mounted; where was Richard? Where were the merry men? And where—oh where—was Anne?

How much time passed in this futile search, I do not know; I had, indeed, almost lost hope when, stopping for a moment before a small but intricately carved door of polished oak, I heard the familiar voice lifted in song from within:

"Thank God," I exclaimed; "we have found her. She is in there."

Mr. Jones appeared skeptical. "Are you sure?" he asked. "I should not like to make a mistake, at this juncture."

"She is cutting her toenails," I explained.

"Come, come," said Mr. Jones. "You are having me on!"

"Not at all, I assure you."

"Really?"

"Really. She is singing 'Land of Hope and Glory.'"

And I added, unhappily,

"I'm afraid she won't hear us knock."

"No matter," said Mr. Jones valiantly. "Not to worry. That is, if you are sure . . ."

And drawing a large key from his pocket, he inserted it in the lock; the door swung open, and we entered the room.

It was, as I had feared, a bedchamber, equipped with a large canopied bed around which the curtains were still drawn. Anne stood near the window, one bare pink and white foot prettily poised above a silver basin; on our entrance, she turned in alarm, gathering her nightrobe around her, but on seeing me she gave an astonished cry, let everything fall, and the next moment she was in my arms. I heard Mr. Jones clear his throat behind me, though whether from emotion or embarrassment, I couldn't tell. Nor did it seem, at the moment, of importance, I was so lost in rapture.

After the first long embrace, she drew back, and gazed at me searchingly. "Euwen," she said; "are you all right?"

"Of course," I said. "I am now, anyway."

"And you didn't drown, or go back to America?"

"No, I didn't," I said.

"I did miss you so much!" she declared.

Again she drew me close; my face was lost in the golden forest of her hair. "Anne," I said; "what about you?"

"I'm all right, darling," she said. "Though," she added honestly, "there *was* nearly a nasty moment."

"Actually," said Mr. Jones, "we haven't time for all this. I suggest that we put it off until later."

"Right," said Anne eagerly. "I shall be dressed in a jiffy." And retiring behind a magnificent carved screen at the far end of the room, she began her toilet.

It took a little longer than I expected, and the day growing steadily brighter, Mr. Jones and I waited in some anxiety and impatience for her to finish. She was already applying make-up to her face, when, to my horror, I heard the unmistakable sound of a snore from behind the drawn curtains of the bed. My first reaction, I must confess, was one of fright; but this was followed almost at once by an access of indignation, and I moved impulsively to draw the curtains apart and to confront whoever was there; but in this I was restrained in time by Mr. Jones, who wisely pointed out that I had no weapon, and that even if I had had one, I shouldn't have known how to use it. He also added that if the snore came from the King, I would surely be hanged for my audacity.

"It is a wise bird," he said, "that lets sleeping

dogs lie. What you don't know, can't hurt you. Consider: there might possibly be no one there. Or there might be the King; or the King's pet poodle. Who knows what a woman takes to bed with her? So what choices do you have? By drawing the curtains, you have nothing to gain, and everything to lose, Niniane's confidence, your own peace of mind, and even, possibly, your neck."

Since he was, of course, right, I withdrew as far as possible from the bed, and stood with my back to it until Anne had finished her toilet, when the three of us left the room, locking the door behind us.

It seemed as though the coast was clear, and I had begun to breathe again, when, halfway down the stairs to the great hall, we found ourselves suddenly confronted by a dozen of the King's men, led by a captain who barred the way with drawn sword. "Well," I said as calmly as I could, "there you are; we are done for. Robin Hood has deserted us."

"The three of you," said the captain, "will return whence you came, until your nature and state can be determined. Meanwhile, you are captives of the King."

"And what King," said Mr. Jones boldly, "is that?"

"Why," said the captain, somewhat taken aback, "King John, of course; as you very well know." And turning to his men, he exclaimed,

"Seize them!"

At this moment, as our fate trembled in the balance, Richard stepped out of the shadows, his helmet in his hand, and a gold circlet on his head. "Forbear, young Percy," he said. "There is no King John. There is only Richard."

Struck with dismay, the captain stood and stared, then slowly bent his knee, and the pikemen, lowering their pikes, followed suit. "It is Richard," they murmured. "Risen from the dead.

"In person."

"Long live the King!"

And young Percy, with bowed head, whispered,

"Forgive us, Sire."

Richard graciously bade him rise. "I do not blame you," he said; "and it is with a heavy heart that I return to my kingly duties. Meanwhile, be so kind as to escort my three friends to the main entrance, and see them safely across the draw."

And turning to Anne, who had dropped a neat curtsy before him, he remarked,

"My dear, I have seen you before; and I have a feeling that I shall see you again. Indeed, as long as there is an England, I shall always see you . . . that milk-white skin, that complexion of honey and roses which is the sign and glory of English womanhood. My own wife was a Cyprian, which can be said to have its advantages; but in the end I find myself always a little homesick for columbine, rosemary, and rue."

Sighing, he patted her cheek. "You have a charming voice," he said; "though untrained, and perhaps a little off key. But that, too, is English. What was it you were singing when you got out of bed?"

" 'Land of Hope and Glory,' your Majesty," said Anne.

He nodded. "A bit of tomorrow's music, I have no doubt."

With that, and with a sweet smile, he dismissed us. The last we saw of him, he was mounting the stairs, humming Blondel's song:

"For to the lover beauty is his love . . ."

The Elixir

Escorted out through the main gate and over the drawbridge by young Percy, we piled into the de Dion, and, after some massive heaves on the crank handle, Mr. Jones got the engine started, and we rolled away from Belvoir Castle, Mr. Jones driving, and Anne and I in the rear seat.

For a while we drove in silence, Anne's head against my shoulder. It was a lovely morning; the mist had burned off, we had left the forest behind, and the shires were before us. The sun shone on the green fields and gently rolling hills, on farm and copse, on distant castles and manors set in their parks. Here was the dreaming heartland of England, set in its peaceful frame, the wealth and might of Empire, the dark, rich soil of history; and over it the light blue sky with its small, swift-moving clouds. Past and present met all around me, fused into a single landscape. The Cotswolds rose blue and distant to the west, and before me, beyond Oxford's Gothic towers, lay London and the BOAC jet.

I should have been happy, and so, in a way, I was. Anne was beside me, the soft warmth of her body cradled in my arm, her fragrance—the fragrance of Summer itself—around me in the air; we had escaped all manner of dangers, we were together. Yet something troubled me; and no matter how I tried to turn my mind away from it, to banish it from my spirit—it refused to be banished. It was the memory of a bed with the curtains drawn . . .

She must have felt something in my manner, for after a while she drew herself away from me, and sat on her side of the seat. "You hate me," she said.

Taken by surprise, it was a moment or two before I burst out laughing. "Why on earth should I hate you?" I demanded. "I love you." But at the same time, I felt a sinking of the heart.

"No," she said stubbornly; "you hate me." But her lip quivered and her eyes filled with tears.

I drew her back, reluctant, into my arms. "I don't hate you," I said; "and you shouldn't talk such nonsense."

"You're going to leave me," she murmured, her head against my breast.

"Only because I have to," I replied. "And as for that—you could come with me."

"To America?"

"Where else?"

Mr. Jones spoke quietly from the front seat. "She has something else waiting for her," he said. "As you must surely know by now."

I nodded dumbly. "I know," I said. And of course I did know. Whoever it was I held in my arms—Anne, Niniane, Nimue—she could never leave England. Because she was England . . .

"The tree people were busy all night long," she said. "Muttering and yattering. But I wasn't afraid . . . much."

"Is that," I inquired, despite myself, "what you meant by a nasty moment?"

She was silent for a moment. "No," she said at last in a low voice.

"I see," I said calmly. But of course, I didn't see, and I felt anything but calm. I didn't want to go on, yet something drove me, some all-too-human perversity. "It's curious," I said, hating myself the while, "that Richard should have mentioned your singing . . . don't you think?"

"It was, rather," she agreed; but she sounded uncertain. "Do you think I sing out of tune, Euwen?" she asked.

"As a matter of fact, I think you sing beautifully," I replied. "Still—that's not the point, is it?"

She didn't answer at once. "No," she said at last. "I don't suppose it is. Actually."

"I mean," I went on relentlessly, "how would he know?"

"I suppose he heard me," she said resignedly, "somewhere."

"When you got out of bed?"

Again a long silence. "You're being rather horrid," she said finally.

Drawing herself away from me once more, she pushed the hair back from her face. "Funnily enough," she said drearily, "Richard wasn't even there last night."

"She is right, you know," said Mr. Jones. "If you remember, his Majesty was with us in the Greenwood. So he couldn't have been."

Of course he was, I thought; and was immediately filled with remorse and with an overwhelming sense of grief. What had I done, with my insane suspicions? Just what Mr. Jones had told me I would do: I had lost everything except my neck. And Anne sat there, looking so pitiable, so vulnerable, with her hands folded hopelessly in her lap—

"Darling," I cried, "can you ever forgive me? I am the lowest of the low."

She turned her face toward me, and gazed at me tenderly. Then, in a quiet, scholarly voice, she declared:

"Romantic love, as we know it today, is based upon the worship of the madonna, or mother-virgin image—a concept brought to Western Europe by returning Crusaders who probably learned it from the Mohammedans to whom the purity (though not necessarily the virginity) of their women was a matter of deep concern. This notion of a pure though ardent and ever-faithful devotion, unknown in the world before the twelfth century A.D., was to dictate the art and morals of the Western world until the present day."

I recognized the gist—if not the actual sense—of this essay as being from a lecture I had heard delivered by Lord Kenneth Clark earlier that year on public television. It is true that later in the same lecture the wise and eminent scholar appeared to have some doubts about his own conclusions, but nevertheless my first impression of Anne as a graduate of Oxford—or Cambridge—returned in full force, and, in my confused state of mind, made me more miserable than before.

Seeing me sitting there mute and, as it were,

thunderstruck, she broke into her sudden bubble of laughter. "Just think," she exclaimed happily, "we've had our second quarrel!"

And nestling once again in my arms, she murmured breathlessly,

"How lovely!"

I realized that, for whatever it was worth, it would have to do. At least, it answered one question, despite the fact that it only left another in its place: If not Richard, then who? And at the same time, I knew that—as Mr. Jones had warned me earlier—it was better not to ask. And I repeated to myself Browning's lines:

> *Where the apple reddens,*
> *Never pry;*
> *Lest we lose our Edens . . .*

and bent to kiss the top of her head.

"Man's mind," declared Mr. Jones from the front seat, "is an extraordinary contraption capable of miraculous feats. Everyone knows that many Asiatic mystics, saints, and sages, have been able to immunize their bodies to pain, and to foretell the day and hour of their deaths. According to Nelson's *Encyclopedia,* published in 1906, the fundamental principle of association is continuity of attention. However, since the flow of ideas is independent of the actual environment, ideal digression is always possible.

"Therefore it is reasonable to assume that the mind can forget what it chooses to forget just as easily as it can remember what it wishes to remember. The point is, of course, that the attention must never be allowed to dwell, even for an instant, on the object or objects, situation, or circumstance which is to be forgotten. This lesson was taught me by no less a person than Mailgrenn himself; you can look him up if you like, in Higgins's *Celtic Druids*, London, 1809.

"In short, what you prefer not to know can be considered nonexistential. Out of sight, out of mind, as it were. What!"

Mr. Jones's advice struck me as being not without merit; indeed, it seemed to make a good deal of sense, and so, putting all thoughts of the past resolutely out of my head, I began to feel much more cheerful and once again filled with wonder at my girl's beauty and spirit.

Romantic love—But what other love is there?

Affection—yes; even devotion, habit, desire; the longing for an heir, and thereby immortality of a sort . . . but all that is only comfort after all, there is no anguish in it and no rapture; and so, no joy. Love alone is the true joy, the—how did Mr. Jones put it?—the continuity of attention. I felt that I could look at Anne forever, and never tire of it, or feel less longing and delight.

And she, in turn, gazed back at me with joy, but with a curious, questioning sadness, as though to say: Why do we have to part?

"We should be coming through Oxford soon," said Mr. Jones. "Give us a song to speed us on our way, Niniane, there's a good girl."

"I have neither lute nor harp," said Anne.

"You'll find your old guitar under the seat," said Mr. Jones. "I thought you might want it."

She reached down and with a cry of delight brought out the guitar. "Ah, my lovely," she said, stroking the polished wood with her fingers, and holding it to her cheek. Then, after tightening the strings, which were badly out of tune, she passed the strap over her shoulder, tried out a few chords, and began to sing:

The Elixir

Early one morning, just as the sun was rising,
I heard a maiden singing in the valley below:
"Oh don't deceive me, Oh never leave me,
How could you use a poor maiden so."

"Very pretty," said Mr. Jones. "Though I thought you might have given us something a bit more in the spirit of the morning."

For myself, I thought it very much in the spirit of the morning, and so, obviously, did Anne, for a spot of color appeared on either cheek. "Very well," she said; "then I shall give you something else"; and almost at once began:

That life that in the morning shone so bright,
Withouten end,
Grows dim and dimmer yet as wanes the light,
And shadows bend.
And what was long withouten end in sight,
Falls short and shorter still as cometh night.
Oh that two lovers should be forced apart,
From sight and sound,
Each with the mortal dagger in his heart,
Time's woeful wound.

"Actually," said Mr. Jones uncomfortably, "what I had in mind was something more like 'Jolly boating weather, with a hay-harvest breeze . . .'"

"Really, Myrdin!" exclaimed Anne indignantly. And with fingers flying, she launched into a version of "The Maid of Amsterdam":

> *In Camelford there lived a maid,*
> *Mark you well what I say.*
> *In Camelford there lived a maid,*
> *And she was mistress of her trade.*
> *I'll go no more a-roving*
> *With mistletoe and rue,*
> *Since roving's been my ruin.*

Myrdin, I thought. Myrdin . . . where had I heard that name before? It sounded strangely like Merlin.

12

Beyond Oxford, whose towers and spires, dreaming in the Summer air, were glimpsed only distantly from across the river, we came to Iffley, and a little farther on passed three young men whom I took to be college students from the cut of their beards, their strange clothes, and high-peaked, slouched hats each sporting a feather. They were carrying a medium-sized barrel between them; it was, apparently, heavy, and they were having some trouble walking. "Shan't we stop," asked Anne in a troubled voice, "and give them a lift?"

Mr. Jones braked the car, and we waited for the three to come up to us, lugging their barrel. "Would you care for a lift?" Mr. Jones asked; at which, to my surprise, instead of eagerly assenting, they appeared to hesitate and to exchange uneasy glances. At length one of them, whom I took to be of foreign descent because of his swarthy complexion, shrugged his shoulders. "Why not?" he said. "We can't very well carry the ruddy thing all the way to London."

"Tresham said he'd have a wagon waiting at Oldham," said one of the others. "Still," he admitted, "that's a long way yet."

"All right, then," said the first man; "up with it; but carefully."

Anne and I climbed down from our places and got into the front with Mr. Jones, and the three men made their way into the rear of the car, and sat down holding the barrel on their laps. "By God," said the youngest of the three, "I never expected to be helped on my way by the Establishment!"

"We are scarcely the Establishment," said Mr. Jones calmly, "although we have been established here for some time. That is to say, Miss—ah—Mellers, and myself, who are both of us from Cornwall. Mr. Irwin, on the other hand, is from America."

The three men then introduced themselves as

Guido, or Guy, Percy, and Catesby. "Are you on your way to London from the university?" asked Mr. Jones.

"As for that," replied Catesby, who appeared to be the oldest and the best dressed, "both yes, and no. Yes to one, that is, and no to the other."

"I assure you," said Mr. Jones, "I had no intent to pry. Your business is your own. But merely out of curiosity, may I inquire what is in that heavy and apparently valuable parcel you are carrying?"

"Pig's food," said Guido shortly.

"Dear me," said Mr. Jones, "I should have thought there were more pigs in Buckinghamshire than in London."

"There are pigs everywhere in the Establishment," said Guido.

Catesby leaned forward, and tapped Mr. Jones on the shoulder. "My good man," he remarked, "did I understand you to say that the gentleman here is from America? Then perhaps he could give us some news of the state of the Catholic party there."

"Why," I said, "I believe the Catholics to be in good health, although I have heard that there is some dispute among them on the subject of discipline."

The three young men exchanged glances at this, and Guido declared,

"There was no such trouble in Portugal."

"But tell me," I said; "you seem to be against the Establishment. Can you tell me what this Establishment is?—for I have never been able to define it."

"Why," said Guido, "that's a simple matter after all. There are two worlds, man—like the world that is in, and the world that is out. One has the power; and the other has injustice; one is corrupt, and at war with nature; the other is sunk in poverty and despair. We believe there is a third world, of order, justice, and peace."

"That would be highly desirable," said Mr. Jones; "and I might add that it is something that I and my friends have long wanted to find. How do you propose to discover it?"

Guido patted the barrel on his knee. "With this," he said.

He added:

"We have many more barrels hidden away, under public buildings, churches, schools, and markets throughout the country. When the time comes, we shall establish our third world."

"By what means?"

"By blowing everything up," said Guido.

To which young Percy added happily,

"Kill the pigs."

"Both of you talk too much," said Catesby. "I don't mind paying for all this, but I am obliged to remind you that I am risking my money to bring this barrel to Westminster."

"And I am risking my neck," said Guido, "or, at best, a trip to Algiers. But one cannot fight corruption with words alone; for one thing, no one listens to you. I am quite ready to lay down my life; but in the meanwhile, I expect you to continue to pay the bills."

"By 'pigs,'" said Mr. Jones, "I take it that you are referring to officers of the Crown. The animal itself, of the breed *sus scrofa* of the family *Surdae*, is, next to men, the most intelligent animal—with the possible exception of the chimpanzee, who can be taught to imitate man's actions without understanding them. The pig, on the other hand, is dignified, reserved, and a fierce fighter when aroused; and has had the good sense, unlike the dog, not to take mankind for friend. Affectionate, I should say, he is not."

Anne, who was becoming more and more upset by the trend of the conversation, now exclaimed,

"What earthly good would it do to blow everything up?" To which Catesby replied with passion,

"Our liberties are interfered with, our demonstrations broken up, our riots put down; we have been arrested, our headquarters raided; we have even been killed while resisting arrest. Or that is what it is called. Our persons are not safe, but open to the rudest search and seizure, and every other indignity. And on top of this, there is the cold war with Ireland which has been going on forever, and a hot war with Spain building up.

"Dangerous diseases require desperate remedies. Milder means have been tried, but without effect. The only answer to neglect and oppression is gunpowder."

"But," cried Anne, "there are many innocent people who will find themselves blown up for no fault of their own."

Catesby shrugged his shoulders. "Whoever is

not with us," he said severely, "is part of the problem."

"That strikes me as rather a beastly point of view, if you ask me," said Anne.

"Nobody asked you, mistress," said Guido. "We are determined to bring down the Establishment by whatever means; and we shall go underground to do it. There will be a Boom here, and a Boom there; presently no one will feel safe; and then we shall take over."

"And who," asked Mr. Jones, "will rule?"

The three once again exchanged glances, in which I thought I detected a certain wariness and lack of ease. "We shall see," muttered Catesby, to which Guido added,

"Each man will make his own laws."

And young Percy exclaimed happily,

"Every man a King!"

"What about women?" asked Anne spiritedly. "They have been oppressed since Eve first ate the apple."

"Lady," said Guido, "we cannot liberate women from their natures. It would not be a Catholic thing to do. Besides—give them gunpowder and there'd be no end to mischief; God's blood, they'd blow themselves up, most likely, and every coffee-house in Christendom!"

"I say," exclaimed young Percy, as we approached White Webb's at Enfield, "isn't that old Tresham up there ahead of us?"

Sure enough, on the road before us loomed a cart with two men, one standing well back in the shadow of the other. "Wait a minute," I said; for it seemed to me that there were other men also, hidden behind the cart, and I thought I caught a glint of what might be a breastplate, or an harquebus.

Catesby, apparently, was of the same opinion, for, leaning forward, he gripped Mr. Jones by the arm, and said sharply,

"Stop the bus."

"By God," exclaimed Guido, shading his eyes to look, "it's Tresham all right, but he's got Monteagle with him."

Percy gave a low whistle. "The devil you say!" he exclaimed. "And some King's men too, if I'm not mistaken."

"I knew it," Catesby groaned. "We have been betrayed." And in an excited voice, he began to give out instructions. "We must separate, and each do what he can. You, Percy, north to rouse North-umberland . . ."

"The old gentleman won't like it," said Percy. "But I shall do my best."

"And you, Fawkes, to the hiding place beneath Westminster. For myself, I shall repair to the cave at Oldham."

And without further delay, the three of them scrambled out of the rear seat onto the roadway. "Shall you not take your barrel with you?" asked Mr. Jones.

"Don't be a ruddy fool," said Guido.

And Catesby added urgently,

"We leave the barrel in your care. The road to London is blocked; therefore head south for Dorset and deliver the barrel to Sir Everard Digby. If he asks you how you came by it, say: 'The weather is bad.' Above all, do not allow yourselves to be taken with it in your possession."

Anne clapped her hands. "Digby!" she cried. "Oh Euwen; we shall be going to Sherborne again." And turning toward Mr. Jones, she added,

"Let us hurry, for I think that some of the harquebuses are pointed this way."

And indeed, the two men, Tresham and Mont-eagle, were advancing in our direction, followed by several men-at-arms, and calling upon us to stand.

Fawkes, Catesby, and Percy had vanished into the hedges lining the road, and—the road being narrow—Mr. Jones had some difficulty in turning the car, but finally achieved it, and just in time, for Tresham's foot was almost on the rear step when we straightened out and headed back toward Iffley, meaning to turn west toward Swindon and south across Salisbury Plain and Blackmoor Vale.

It is a fact that in the excitement I had com-pletely forgotten London and the waiting jet; the thought of being once again with Anne at the Dog and Duck put all other thoughts out of my mind; in imagination I relived those magical days and nights at the Sword and Crown above the cliffs at Tintagel Head, and flushed and smiling, I reached for her hand, to find her as warm and eager as myself.

"Step on it!" I cried to Mr. Jones; and Anne breathed happily,

"Hurry!"

We had need to hurry; for at Iffley a company of men-at-arms was already drawn up across the road, and would have blocked our way, if Mr. Jones had not spied an opening in a lane, and, turning sharply, soon brought us to yet another lane whose high hedges, sweet with wildflowers, hid us from pursuit. Turning again, at the lane's end, we bumped our way across a field toward where we thought the Great West Road must be. A hunt was in progress; the hounds streaked around us and under us, and a number of ladies in black riding habits and gentle-men in pink coats streamed past us at a furious gallop, one lady actually lifting her mount in a soaring leap directly over the car. "That would be Lady Crumble, most likely," said Anne, "she must be seventy at least. A marvelous old lady. And this must be the Taunton Vale Hunt, so we must be in Somerset. I rode with them once, while Peter was Master of the North Dorset. Mostly, of course, I rode with the West Kent. Once my horse refused a gate, and I was tossed, and the Prince picked me up, all unconscious."

"What Prince was that?" I asked idly.

"Wales," she said simply; "what else? Fortu-nately, I had been presented to him at a garden party the year before; and Nanny had made me wear a clean camisole."

Yes, I thought with delight, nothing has changed; it is just the way it was before. Soon she will make up some enchanting story about her childhood.

"There was another marvelous old lady with the Taunton Vale," she said, "who ate nothing but bonbons and kept falling off her horse. As a matter of fact, she always carried a change of clothes; and would turn up, all covered with muck, at the most unlikely houses, and ask would they mind if she used their bath."

But she didn't really want to talk very much; and as the afternoon gave way to evening, and twilight drew on, she grew more and more silent. She leaned against me as warmly as before, but her expression was thoughtful and even somber. "I love you, Euwen," she murmured once; "try to remember that." And a while later, I heard her singing to herself, under her breath,

"Doom moves in the cold stone."

The evening mist was rising on Salisbury Plain. Far off, too far to be seen, Stonehenge lifted its inscrutable circle to the night. "I feel a doom coming on,

Euwen," she said. "Something is ending."

"The chase is ending," I said comfortingly. "We'll be at Sherborne by daylight."

She sighed, and shook her head. "I shall never see Sherborne again," she said.

"It's strange," she said after a while: "I feel as I did before Arthur's last battle. The world is going back to the way it was: each man a fortress against all others. There is not much time left."

"No," agreed Mr. Jones; "there is not, as a matter of fact."

"I think I can sleep a little, Euwen," she said. "Hold me."

We drove on in silence through the night. I held Anne in my arms, and she slept, her head against my shoulder. At one point it seemed to me that I heard the sound of galloping horses somewhere behind us, faint cries, a clash of trumpets and drums; but it was all far away, and I wasn't sure; it could have been night birds and the wind over the barrows. And I thought about life and death and love: how life wasn't much, really, either then or now—a few years; but that love was a great deal.

Like the Spring, she had said to me once: always new, and yet always the same. And this girl in my arms—this woman whom I loved—she too was like the Spring, forever the same and forever new, in herself all women, yet singular; all my loves, yet separate and alone.

Mr. Jones, also, was silent; I felt that his thoughts were troubled, that he, too, was uncertain, embarked on a journey whose outcome he knew and dreaded, yet could not avoid. Had he heard the galloping of horses behind us? I didn't know.

In the early dawn we came to a body of water, and Mr. Jones stopped the car. "You must rouse her," he said. "We have come to the end of our journey."

I looked around me in surprise. We were at the edge of a quiet lake still shadowed by night, untouched by the sun. A small boat was moored in the weeds of the shore, a skiff or shallop, its oars resting idly in the water. Across the water, in the middle of the lake, I could see a wooded island; the rising sun shone gold in the tops of the trees, and gilded the steeple of a small church or chapel, while leaving deep shadows below. Birds were singing, and a bell tolled three times across the water. Faintly in the distance somewhere behind us, the horses still galloped.

"Surely," I said, "this is not Sherborne Castle?"

"No," he said. "But wake her nevertheless. She will know where she is."

I woke her with a kiss, and she clung to me for a moment, her eyes still closed. But then she roused herself, and I heard her give a gasp. "Merlin," she whispered; "where have you taken us?"

"To Saffron Orcas," said Mr. Jones.

She gazed about her, and her face grew solemn and sad; the proud, fair head, usually held so high, slowly sank. "Yes," she said at last in a low voice, "you have found it, haven't you."

Mr. Jones nodded. "The journey is over, Nimue," he said; "it is time to leave Euwen. Though you and I still have a bit of a way to go."

She sat still for a moment, like a trapped bird. "So it has come," she said. "I was afraid of that."

"I have done all that you asked of me," said Mr. Jones. And he added, his voice trembling a little,

"I have waited a long time."

"I know," said Anne. "Thank you."

"Well then," said Mr. Jones. And drawing a pistol from his pocket, he trained it on me, while with his free hand he helped Anne to dismount from the car. "We are obliged to leave you here, Mr. Irwin," he said. "And to make sure, I will just fasten you to the seat with this leather thong."

"But the King's men will take him!" expostulated Anne.

"I expect they will," replied Mr. Jones calmly; "unless some random shot from a musket, striking the barrel of gunpowder, should blow him up first. Actually, it makes little difference which century he is blown up in. As for me, I am only doing what history demands of me—or, if not history, then legend. There is nothing fundamentally mean in my nature. Have you any last words you would like to say to him, my dear?"

Anne turned on me her wide, lovely eyes, made even more beautiful by sorrow and resignation. "It is true, my darling," she declared. "If I have really come to Saffron Orcas, then I must leave the world of living men and women for the world of my childhood. Only Merlin could have found it for me; I wish with all my heart that he had not. For I have loved you very much—the I who was, for this moment in time—Anne; but who was, before that, Niniane, and before that, Nimue.

"I am ready, Merlin."

So saying she stepped delicately into the shallop, and Mr. Jones, pushing off from shore, began to row her away. The sun rose, and the water, which had been the color of the sky, turned a deeper blue, and the little boat seemed to fill with a golden light. Anne raised one hand in farewell; and I closed my eyes in anguish.

The morning air around me was full of summer sounds, the chirping of birds, the droning of bees, the tolling of the bell from across the lake, the lapping of lake water; and louder and louder, the gallop of horses. Behind my closed eyelids, I could almost see them coming closer and closer; they were around me, jostling, trampling . . . the King's men . . . but what King? Whose voice was that I heard? —or did I hear it?—

"You, Sir Bedivere—Gawaine! Sir Kay."

"Are we too late?"

"Too late, Sire."

I felt the car begin to rock, back and forth, back and forth . . . hands (whose hands?) were on it.

I wanted to cry out "Careful! Be careful! You will blow us all up!"

But it was I myself who was being rocked, ever so gently; and a voice said:

"Fasten your seat belt, please. We have begun our approach to Kennedy International Airport."

CHAPTER

13

"But how," I asked the Dean of Studies at Middleton College, "did you know?"

Seated at his desk in his office above the campus, Dean Briggs gave me a reassuring smile. "It is true," he said, "that when you failed to return in time for the opening of term, we feared that something might have happened to you; possibly, even, that you might have been in one of those planes that were hijacked to the desert. But then we had this letter, to set our minds at rest."

And he passed across the desk an envelope with an English stamp, addressed to the Dean of Studies, Middleton College, Massachusetts, U. S. A. The letter read:

Dear Sir,

This is to inform you that Professor Euwen, having suffered a slight accident, is resting comfortably at the residence of the Apothecary at Camelford in Cornwall, and will be a few days late in returning to his duties at your institution.

> I am, sir
>
> Your humble servant,
>
> M. Jones.

"Curious," said the Dean, "that he should call you Euwen. A slip of the pen, perhaps; or have I misread his writing?"

I gave the letter back to him. "This Mr. Jones," he asked, "was he a friend of yours?"

"Yes," I said. "Of a sort."

"Well," said the Dean uncertainly, "you must come to tea some day with Mrs. Briggs and myself, and tell us all about it."

"Thank you," I said. "I will." And I thought to myself, as I rose to go,

I shall have to make up something.

Midsummer hung heavy over Middleton. The campus was filled with the usual boys and girls in their faded Levis, bright-colored sweaters and blouses, battlejackets, ballooning, gaily striped trousers, torn shirts with their shirttails hanging out . . . beards, beads, and flowers, long hair, bare legs. They looked familiar enough; I had been seeing them, one way or another, for a thousand years.

I returned to my classes, to the teaching of history—the dates and the facts and the realities. Young people want to be told the truth—or what they take to be the truth. "Tell it like it is," they say. "Tell it like it was."

How can I tell it like it was? Can I tell them that today and yesterday are equal parts of a tapestry; that nothing is what it looks to be, and that to close the mind to appearances is to open it to wonder? And that one can fall in love with a legend?

❀   ❀   ❀

The Summer days move slowly across the sky. At night, in my little house off-campus, among the trees, I draw the blinds against the tree people. And sometimes, in the quiet dark, I think I hear Anne singing:

> *Long gone, the kiss of heart and tongue,*
> *And Eleanor in her beautie,*
> *Long gone, long gone.*

I am, perhaps, a little sad at times, but I am not unhappy. Anne is with me in a way that I cannot describe. I keep thinking of the Old Man of the Mountain: "It is all one, because it has happened. Whatever is, has been, and always will be."

Whatever has been, is, and always will be. I tell myself that.

Funnily enough, I am to have an assistant in the Fall. I have been told that she is young, that she received her doctorate at Oxford, and that her dissertation was entitled: "Merlin's England, Myth and Reality."

BOOKS BY
ROBERT NATHAN
PUBLISHED BY ALFRED A. KNOPF

Novels

THE ELIXIR (*1971*)

MIA (*1970*)

STONECLIFF (*1967*)

THE MALLOT DIARIES (*1965*)

THE FAIR (*1964*)

THE DEVIL WITH LOVE (*1963*) A STAR IN THE WIND (*1962*)

THE WILDERNESS-STONE (*1961*)

THE COLOR OF EVENING (*1960*) SO LOVE RETURNS (*1958*)

THE RANCHO OF THE LITTLE LOVES (*1956*)

SIR HENRY (*1955*) THE TRAIN IN THE MEADOW (*1953*)

THE INNOCENT EVE (*1951*) THE MARRIED LOOK (*1950*)

THE ADVENTURES OF TAPIOLA (*1950*)

(*containing* JOURNEY OF TAPIOLA, *1938*,

and TAPIOLA'S BRAVE REGIMENT, *1941*)

THE RIVER JOURNEY (*1949*) LONG AFTER SUMMER (*1948*)

MR. WHITTLE AND THE MORNING STAR (*1947*)

BUT GENTLY DAY (*1943*) THE SEA-GULL CRY (*1942*)

THEY WENT ON TOGETHER (*1941*)

PORTRAIT OF JENNIE (*1940*) WINTER IN APRIL (*1938*)
THE BARLY FIELDS (*1938*)

(*containing* THE FIDDLER IN BARLY, *1926*,

THE WOODCUTTER'S HOUSE, *1927*,

THE BISHOP'S WIFE, *1928*, THE ORCHID, *1931*,

and THERE IS ANOTHER HEAVEN, *1929*)

THE ENCHANTED VOYAGE (*1936*) ROAD OF AGES (*1935*)

ONE MORE SPRING (*1933*) JONAH (*1925*)

Poems

THE MARRIED MAN (*1962*) THE GREEN LEAF (*1950*)
THE DARKENING MEADOWS (*1945*)
MORNING IN IOWA (*1944*) DUNKIRK (*1941*)
A WINTER TIDE (*1940*) SELECTED POEMS (*1935*)

Theater

JULIET IN MANTUA (*1966*)
JEZEBEL'S HUSBAND & THE SLEEPING BEAUTY (*1953*)

For Young People

TAPPY (*1968*)
THE SNOWFLAKE AND THE STARFISH (*1959*)

Archaeology

THE WEANS (*1960*)

These are BORZOI BOOKS, *published in New York
by* ALFRED A. KNOPF

A NOTE ABOUT THE AUTHOR

Robert Nathan was born in New York City in 1894 and was educated at private schools in the United States and Switzerland. While attending Harvard University he was an editor of the Harvard Monthly, *in which his first stories and poems appeared. Except for two short periods, during which he was a solicitor for a New York advertising firm and a teacher in the School of Journalism of New York University, Mr. Nathan has devoted his time exclusively to writing. He is the author of over fifty volumes of poetry and prose, and from this body of distinguished work he has acquired a reputation as a master of satiric fantasy unique in American letters. A member of the National Institute of Arts and Letters since 1935, Mr. Nathan has made his home in California for the past twenty-seven years, and lives in Los Angeles with his English-born actress-wife, Anna Lee.*

A NOTE ON THE TYPE

The text of this book is set in Caledonia, a Linotype face designed by W. A. Dwiggins (1880–1956), the man who was responsible for so much that is good in contemporary book design and typography. Caledonia belongs to the family of printing types called "modern face" by printers—a term used to mark the change in style of type-letters that occurred about 1800. It has all the hard-working feet-on-the-ground qualities of the Scotch Modern face plus the liveliness and grace that is integral in every Dwiggins "product" whether it be a simple catalogue cover or an almost human puppet.

This book was composed, printed, and bound by Kingsport Press, Inc., Kingsport, Tennessee.